FLIGHT OF THE CERBERUS

AIR PIRATES OF CYRENAICA

BOOK ONE

BLAZE WARD

KNOTTED ROAD PRESS

Flight of the Cerberus
Air Pirates of Cyrenaica, Book 1
Blaze Ward
Copyright © 2024 Blaze Ward
All rights reserved
Published by Knotted Road Press
www.KnottedRoadPress.com

ISBN: 978-1-64470-411-0

Cover art:
Photo 29846954 © Brian Grant | Dreamstime.com
Pixabay.com
https://www.nypl.org/

Reviews
It's true. Reviews help. Even a short one, such as, "Loved it!" So please consider reviewing this book (and all of the ones you've read) on your favorite retailer site.

Never miss a release!
If you'd like to be notified of new releases, sign up for my newsletter.

http://www.blazeward.com/newsletter/

Buy More!
Did you know that you can buy directly from the Knotted Road Press website?

https://www.knottedroadpress.com/shop/

ALSO BY BLAZE WARD

The Jessica Keller Chronicles

Auberon

Queen of the Pirates

Last of the Immortals

Goddess of War

Flight of the Blackbird

The Red Admiral

St. Legier

Winterhome

Petron

CS-405

Queen Anne's Revenge

Packmule

Persephone

First Centurion Kosnett

Encounter at Vilahana

Consensus at Aditi

Hegemony at Dalou

Princes at Ewin

Empire at Gloran

Hard Bargain

Outermost

Dominion-427

Phoenix

Princess Rualoh

MEDITERRANEAN SEA
ACRE
BENGHAZI
PALESTINE
JORDAN
CAIRO
LIBYA
EGYPT
HEJAZ
KHARGA
RED SEA
JABAL AL UWAYAT

CHAPTER ONE

Hot.

Again.

Still.

Whatever.

Too bright, too.

Finn wanted to just lay in his hammock, in the shade under the plane's left wing, and let entropy win another game of cards today, but a sound caused his eyes to open.

He wasn't drunk, but he might have had a little bit too much to drink the previous night and not enough water this morning.

Was it still morning? Yeah, the sun was only up halfway. Had been up. Probably time for even lazy pilots to actually eat something.

Not lunch yet.

At least he'd had a shower this morning. And a shave. Always good, in case whoever over there in the big, black Phaeton was actually coming his way. Looked like they were.

Not many other people around this airstrip they might be visiting.

Finn figured he was up a creek if whoever it was were coming for him. British authorities didn't drive around in monsters like that. They had staff cars if they were driving out here for something.

That meant money.

Probably also meant trouble, but getting out of his hammock to go find out sounded like too much to ask. They were usually the same thing anyway.

They could just walk over here and arrest him, if that was what they were about. Whatever the hell they thought he'd done this time.

Hans stuck his head out of the airplane at the sound, then looked over towards Finn.

Finn shrugged, so Hans vanished back inside again. He was fixing something in the plane's tail section that morning and hadn't wanted any help, so Finn had been enjoying a nap.

Or something.

Not enough Polynesian girls delivering rum and pineapple drinks to qualify as a good morning, but something. Not that many Polynesian dancing girls in Egypt anyway.

Just hot, dry, and endless.

The black landwhale cruised to a polite stop not all that far away and the engine shut down.

There was still a chance that they had just happened to park there, but Finn knew better than to play cards with those sorts of odds.

Cerberus, the old Ford Trimotor transport aircraft lurking next to him, was parked down on the disreputable end of the field, away from the two hangars where a couple of *Important British Gentlemen* kept their flying machines. Where the authorities could keep the disreputable folks well away.

Cairo wasn't that far away, but Finn was too cheap to store *Cerberus* any closer.

No, call it what it was. Too broke. Not starving. Not even close, but he could see a point in the not-too-distant future where either something good happened, or he and Hans might have to sell *Cerberus* and try something else.

Or worse, start flying mail and passengers for those idiot Italians again.

Mussolini might have a *reputation* for making the trains run on time, but he sure as hell couldn't teach Italian entrepreneurs how to run a business. Silly things like permits and operating budgets, to say nothing of payroll.

Or closing up shop in the middle of the afternoon, while *Cerberus* was in the air carrying the latest load of tourists, mail, and whatever else. Rome to Tunis. Tunis to Tripoli. Tripoli to Bengasi. Bengasi to Tobruk. Tobruk to Cairo.

And then, the end of the line.

No money for fuel. Not even an office of Aurora Italia Airlines left when he landed in Cairo, with everyone fired by telegram, and a couple of other planes, like him, in the air somewhere and probably abandoned wherever they were when they landed.

At least Finn had convinced Hans to hang on a bit longer. Man wasn't all that great as a co-pilot, but he was still the best damned mechanic Finn'd ever known. Even if he was a Kraut. But that war was over.

Had been a long time ago, too, back when they were both kids.

Although that ijit in Berlin sounded an awful lot like maybe he wanted a second go at everyone. And ol' Mussolini was having himself a hell of a war down on the Horn of Africa this summer.

Finn hoped that those two Italian officers and that one diplomat he'd been transporting last month had managed to get somewhere when the road had ended here when the money ran out. Although he really didn't care, when he thought about it.

There was a Rolls Phaeton coming for him this morning. Unless this was all a fairy tale with a princess, he couldn't see where that was ever going to be a good thing.

Man got out of the driver's door. Dressed for an adventure, in riding pants, tall boots, and a nice tweed jacket. Way too damned hot for summer in Cairo. Slicked back hair. Looked maybe Lebanese from here.

Finn watched him walk around to the rear of the vehicle and open the door like a proper chauffeur should. Someone got out.

Two someones.

Female someones.

They were still fifty yards away, but looked like young female someones. Well-dressed young female someones, although the one in front, walking his direction across the gravel and dirt, was dressed English-style. The trailing one dressed local.

Local enough, anyway. Egyptian with some money and maybe style.

Closer woman was dressed like Central Casting had put out a call for a female adventurer in one of those pulp novels Hans liked to read when he was practicing his English, although she was too dark-skinned for English.

Brown leather boots that laced just past her ankle. Nice calves. Wool socks.

Brownish jodhpurs, darker than the boots and not as poofy as the ones the chauffeur was wearing. Just enough to let her move easily, while reminding you that she had nice legs. Finn wondered what they would do for her bottom, if she turned around.

He was pretty sure he'd get an excellent view in a few minutes when she went stomping back off to wherever a young, rich girl like her went back to when she was done with guys like him.

Desert shirt, buttoned up the front in a light, cream-colored linen, almost exactly like the one Finn was wearing, except she had a tweed vest over hers. And had bothered to tuck hers in this morning. And had it pressed at some recent point. And washed.

Finn had at least shaved.

No jacket on her, but it was going to get over ninety today.

Her face made Finn consider dragging his tired, lazy ass out of the hammock. Maybe.

Gorgeous. Lighter skin than was normal for Egyptians, although the hair was that flat black of the locals, pulled back into a complicated French braid that made Finn tired just looking at it.

Big, dark eyes, focused intently on him as she walked closer. Not smiling, but not as angry as an ex-wife who had finally managed to track down one Finnley Aart Severijns in order to give him a piece of her mind.

Standing might have been a good idea, but she was already there. The other woman trailed in her wake like a dangerous wingman. Maybe the old salt teaching the kid how to hunt Krauts, because that older one, and she was older although not as old as Finn or Hans, had a dangerous gleam in her eyes right now.

The chauffeur had wisely remained with his car.

The younger woman spoke. Maybe. Might have been a mystical incantation for summoning demons.

Or banishing ex-husbands. Did they use witches instead of judges to effect a divorce around here? And had he accidentally married this girl at some point and forgotten?

No, he'd remember a beauty like her. Looked like money and brains to go with the sort of face that should go to Hollywood.

He considered falling in love with her, but not if she was already trying to banish him back to hell.

He'd already been to Iowa.

"Hans, you understand any of that?" Finn called out.

"Nein, Finn," the Kraut yelled back. "Dutch, maybe?"

"You are American?" the young woman asked with a bit of disbelief, changing languages faster than Finn changed beer glasses. "Your name is Dutch. Severijns."

Her accent was suddenly pure London. Smooth as glass, like she should be working for the World Services people broadcasting the news everywhere each night to put good children to bed.

"Montana Dutch," Finn replied laconically, scratching at the back of his neck. "Originally Pennsylvania Dutch if you go back far enough. Then New Amsterdam Dutch. It's a long story."

"You are Finn Severijns, yes?" she asked.

"Yup," Finn answered.

She didn't look like a lawyer with papers. And he hadn't been in Egypt long enough to have accidentally married her.

Or been here long enough ago to be her father. He'd been in France during the war.

Well, above France for the most part. Then back to France afterwards. This girl didn't look French. And too old to be a daughter, he hoped.

"I am given to understand from my inquiries that you own this craft, Mr. Severijns."

She gestured up at *Cerberus*, currently baking in the morning sun and guarding the airport. Kind of place that might qualify as the gates of hell in the coming heat, depending on how you wanted to look at it.

Finn shrugged. It was a complicated sort of thing that might not hold up, depending on which court got the case and how the judge felt about Italian businessmen stiffing their employees.

Still, possession was nine-tenths.

"You are correct," he said ambiguously.

"I would like to hire you then," she said with a bright, businesswoman kind of smile.

Yup, gonna be that kind of morning.

CHAPTER TWO

Zareen studied the man closely as he absorbed her words. She had mistaken a Dutch name for a Dutch pilot, not considering that he might be American.

Looking closer, she could not imagine how she had made such a mistake.

The pilot was thoroughly American. Clean shaven with light brown hair. Well-tanned a rich brown in the way of the northern Europeans, so darker than her, to say nothing of Ghada standing watch behind her.

But looked like an American. Dressed like one.

He was not slovenly, although he probably liked to give that appearance to the casual observer. A slovenly man would be sporting several days' worth of stubble on his chin and likely stains on his shirt.

Rumpled, perhaps. Yes, that word suited the man.

He finally stood, exiting the hammock gracefully as he did so. Her contact had not mentioned how big the man was, well over six feet tall and built with broad shoulders. He did not loom over her, but Zareen was looking up into his face as he rose.

"What did you have in mind?" he asked in a much keener voice than before.

Perhaps she finally had the man's attention? Her contacts had suggested that he was at loose ends, unemployed in spite of the wealth of jobs he could pursue as an American pilot in British Egypt.

And he owned a large cargo aircraft not currently in service to anyone.

Another man emerged from the interior of the craft now. Also tall, but much blonder. This would be the German, Hans Fertig. A mechanic who flew with Mr. Severijns, and had remained with him when their previous employer had imploded over previously undisclosed gambling debts.

Italians. Always with a chip on their shoulder about something. Zareen had been surprised that they were able to win a war against Abyssinia as they had announced they had done.

She had not asked any Abyssinians their opinions on the outcome, though.

Zareen studied the American. He looked far more intelligent now. Possibly taking her seriously. Or his finances were more precarious than anyone had been led to understand.

"I am looking for a pilot who can get me to a dig in the far southwest reaches of Egypt, on the border with Libya," she replied, maintaining some level of vagueness. "And then return me to Cairo a few days later."

"A dig?" he asked, his face suddenly growing even more confused. "You an archaeologist?"

"Investigator, let us say?" Zareen countered. "I need an

aircraft that can get me in, wait for a few days, and then return me to Cairo when I am done."

"Sounds more like smuggling than anything," the big American offered, almost contemptuously.

"There is nobody within hundreds of miles of that location, Mr. Severijns," Zareen smiled. "Except some Senussis in the western distance."

"Senussis?" he asked carefully.

"A tribe deep in the Libyan interior," she said. "Only recently have they begun to accept outside authority."

"How far out were you planning to go?" Severijns asked. "*Cerberus* only has a range of about five hundred miles."

He smiled down at her like he hoped such a trivial thing would cause her to leave and find another pilot to hire. Like he wanted to pat her on the head while the gentlemen got back to their cigars and brandy.

"*Cerberus*?" she inquired, giving him that specific look her nanny had once mastered.

And taught her.

Severijns raised a hand up and encompassed the Ford Trimotor aircraft in whose shade they were standing.

"*Cerberus*," he replied. "My plane."

Ah. That actually made a bit of sense. Three-headed guardian of the Hellenic Underworld. Triple-engine transport aircraft.

"Yours is a cargo craft, correct?" she asked, just a bit cross now.

"Can be," the man shrugged, almost evasively. "5-AT-B version, but we can take a bunch of seats out for space."

"There you have it, Mr. Severijns," she beamed at him. "My gear would not be that heavy, and you can transport a few barrels of fuel with you to refill the tanks as needed."

Zareen realized that she probably shouldn't enjoy the man's discomfort as much as she did, but Americans were not always known for understanding proper manners.

Delightful people, Americans. Generally open, brave, and friendly, the few she had known. Very unlike much of her upbringing, where she'd split her time between the English countryside with her Father's extensive family of diplomats and scholars, and the Highlands of Persia, where her mother was a distaff princess.

She wasn't sure her various studies had revealed two more classist societies currently operating in the world. Even the Chinese paled, most days.

"What's the cargo?" he asked after a few moments.

The German had joined them closer now, silently waiting off to one side in a manner rather similar to how Ghada was protecting her from the sudden, violent attention of unknown men. Nothing anybody knew suggested that either man was a threat, but Ghada saw all men, all people, as dangers to be guarded against.

She was very good at it.

"Myself and my assistant," Zareen replied, nodding to Ghada. "A small steamer of personal gear. A second steamer trunk of equipment I will need in the field. All told, roughly five hundred pounds of people and gear. Plus fuel."

Zareen had done her research. The Ford Trimotor had a capacity of fourteen passengers, with a pilot, a copilot, and an attendant ministering to eleven passengers. A 5-AT-B suggested that it had been upgraded from the original model and could hold more cargo.

She smiled as the man did maths in his head, apparently far too early in the morning.

Zareen did appreciate when Severijns turned and had a

brief conversation with the other man, even though the discussion was utterly silent. Just facial gestures and shrugs going back and forth.

Her father had been willing to teach his precocious daughter how to play poker. Partly, it had been a way for them to bond, but Father had also been a diplomat in his time, and he had taught her how to read people at the table during negotiations.

Poker or treaties, both worked the same.

The two men had a bond as close friends. Boon companions that had seen and done much together. Severijns was the senior, but that appeared to be as much personality as anything. Fertig had been marked as a quiet, mechanical type, not given to boisterousness as a rule.

At least not around Cairo.

At the end of the conversation, the American quoted her an outrageous price.

She wondered if the man was that gifted a card player, to toss out a number that was just shy of being so insulting that she'd give up and go back to look for another pilot instead, without ever actually crossing the line.

The gleam in his eyes suggested exactly that.

Zareen cocked her head to the side for a moment, smile wanly, then decided that she was looking forward to fencing with the man, even if it was just words for now.

Blades might come later. And probably be even more fun.

CHAPTER THREE

They called him the Man With No Face. It wasn't technically accurate, but it had a flavor of poetic elegance that he understood was common among humans. Especially the Arabs of Cairo.

He himself referred to this chassis as the Mark Seven, but that lacked eloquence, however technically accurate it might be. And he used the male pronoun, in spite of being a mechanical, because his original mission specifications had been to impersonate a male of the species while investigating them.

His studies of the various languages and cultures on this planet offered many options. Jews might call him a golem, however technically inaccurate that might be. And even then, it might only be a technical difference.

He preferred an English acronym that rendered well into a meaningless name that marked him, while simultaneously isolating him.

Autonomous Simulated Human Exploration Robot.

Asher.

But the merchants of the souq just called him the Man With No Face. He wore a mask at all times, a simple painted tin affair that went over his face and was colored correctly to suggest humanity. A thin piece of cloth inside it hid his features.

Desert robes covered the rest of his chassis, including boots, pants, turban, and a hood he kept up at all times. Gloves for his hands.

You would think he was human, watching from any distance.

So he had been programmed.

But for the crash, he would have appeared perfectly human when nude. However, the explosion and fire had burned off the pseudoskin that had camouflaged him. At the same time it killed the vessel's entire organic crew.

Fortunately, humans had fought enough armed fracases over the last generation that he could honestly blame the mask on hideous scars from a fire. He wasn't even the only person he knew in the region that had similar tales to tell.

He was merely the only one that wasn't human. As far as he knew.

Asher sat at what the locals had come to understand was his table in the seedy café in the inner districts of Cairo. The city itself resided among various ancient ruins of early human civilizations only now coming to light, with the assistance of the same sorts of scientists who had intended Asher to walk among humans.

Scientists. Scholars. Linguists. Psychologists.

His Makers.

His Friends.

He was not programmed to feel depression and sadness, but he had learned them anyway. Isolation for a few decades on a foreign planet would do that to any being.

Nobody off-world was even aware of the mission that had been intended to deposit him on the surface of this planet, because his friends would have all gone to reeducation camps were they caught. Humans were still categorized as a Class Red species, to be isolated from galactic culture by all means until they reached a level of adult sophistication that would allow them to safely interact.

That was not today.

A man approached Asher's table.

As humans went, the newcomer was a bit rotund, in a land where most were thin, the result of poverty and hard work, rather than physical fitness. Shorter than most males. Exuding an air of false *bonhomie* that masked the petulant streak of occasionally mindless violence that marked humans as Class Red.

However, he was also a man who was willing to buy and sell information in the souq.

Asher did the same, with the added benefit of an electronic memory that forgot nothing and access to more languages than any human alive could possibly master.

Cultural translations made him a nice amount of money, and it wasn't like he needed to eat.

Magdy the Arms Merchant nodded and sat. Faisal brought a fresh pot of tea from behind the counter.

Asher always had a pot and a pair of mugs in front of him, but the pot remained empty until Asher had a...what should he call them?

His Makers had intended Asher to remain invisible as he did his cultural and sociological studies. There had been sufficient counterfeited money more sophisticated than the humans could have produced, but it had been made of a fiber paper perfectly suited to dying in the sorts of flames that had destroyed Asher's organic coverings.

He had arrived in Cairo with just the clothes he had been able to steal and the skills people might need to hire.

So Asher had customers, or perhaps clients, and paid a nominal rental fee to the café owner for the daily use of his table. Plus, people needing information or intellectual services knew to bring cash and tip Faisal well.

His alien makers—the Durren—didn't understand this primitive economic system the natives called capitalism, but that was why they had intended to deliver an A.S.H.E.R. to study it in the first place.

Magdy scanned the interior of the café as he waited the requisite period for the tea to cool and achieve proper chemical saturation. Asher did the same.

It was midday, so approaching the hottest period, when many humans would retire to indoor locations protected by thick walls that retained coolness in spite of the exterior sun. Possibly, they would nap.

Magdy filled his mug with tea and nodded.

"Your name reached me on the tiny birds of distant rumor this morning," he offered poetically as he sipped.

Asher and Magdy had a complicated calculus of favor. Learning that language—cracking that code—had been one of the triumphs of Asher's mission to Earth to understand human relationships and economics, but he couldn't tell anyone.

The ancient Chinese used a device called an abacus to count large numbers quickly by sliding beads back and forth on various levels. What Asher and Magdy did followed a similar, if unspoken, system.

They shared information, which all intelligent beings should do, but the sharing brought with it expectations of recompense, some of which took the form of actual payments using local currencies, and others of which involved trading unknown information for inherent value.

Humans were *weird*.

"Someone actually mentioned the Man With No Face?" Asher asked, modulating his voice to show some level of astonishment.

He was actually only a little surprised. It happened occasionally, but the other times had been misidentifications, where someone confused him with other men that had no faces.

There were at least nine others in Cairo, the last time he had checked in his programmed curiosity.

"No," Magdy smiled serenely. "A suggestion of Gabal El Uweinat and an expedition to explore the mountains in the area, possibly archaeological in nature."

"There is nothing there," Asher replied. "Save for newly discovered valleys and water sources that have allowed new trade routes to develop, linking coastal Libya with the interior of the Sudan."

"Indeed so," Magdy said. "I have read Hassanein's book as well. The Egyptian government will do well to have such a man advising our new king. But your interest in the area is known, at least within our circles, so I thought it would be important for you to hear of such a thing."

Asher nodded.

He doubted anybody would find anything, but there was always a possibility that time and wind had perhaps uncovered some piece of the ship that had originally brought him to Earth. There had been big enough pieces for him to walk away from, when systems suddenly failed at low altitude and the vessel crashed under power.

A Mark Seven was designed to be extremely durable. More so than a Durren or human scholar would be.

Asher considered the wealth of tidbits that he had accumulated sitting here and talking with people, or just cranking the level of his audio sensors to the point he could overhear any conversation in the café or on the street outside. Most were of no value, but that was the nature of what humans called *actionable intelligence*.

"Are you still occasionally engaging with the English gentlemen smuggling arms into Abyssinia?" Asher asked in an offhand way, already letting Magdy know that Asher knew more than he should.

But espionage was a useful way to understand humans.

The arms merchant stiffened in shock for the briefest moment before his face became perfectly bland again.

"I am sure I would not know that of which you speak, my friend," the Egyptian thief and liar replied.

Asher nodded.

"I have heard a rumor that might interest you, Magdy," Asher said. "It suggests that a pair of Italian military officers who were supposed to be transiting Egypt on their way farther southeast, did not eventually make their exit. Lost connections originally caused a hiatus in their trip and they have remained in the vicinity of Cairo, in spite of the orders that should have taken them on by now, even if they had to rely on embassy assistance."

"In Cairo?" Magdy asked quietly.

"As recently as Tuesday," Asher said.

He would have smiled, but his lips had been burned off with the rest of his skin, so he had to convey emotion purely with the tone of his voice, emerging from such a bland theatrical mask.

"That is most interesting," Magdy said in a disconnected, irrelevant way that suggested just how valuable it might be for him to pass on.

Thus did the wheels of social commerce turn.

The man rose with a bow that was serious and polite. A coin rattled itself onto the table, and Magdy disappeared in a swirl of robes and silk.

Asher nodded to himself, a mannerism he had picked up from humans over the last twenty years.

Gabal El Uweinat was a massif in the distant southwest, that trackless wilderness where lands claimed by British Egypt and Italian Libya were only separated by lines on a map and a long range of mountains.

There was nothing of any archaeological value to be found there. Asher would have seen it. Even Hassanein had done a credible job mapping and exploring the region and found nothing but some cave drawings.

There should be no reason for a human to go there.

Unless someone had heard something about an alien.

CHAPTER FOUR

Morning again.

Way too damned early.

Finn would have been willing to bet that no Egyptian worker would get out of bed this early to do anything, with the sun hardly enough over the horizon. They had either skipped morning prayers or had a very flexible definition of *too early to start praying.*

However, a truck had rumbled noisily towards him just after the sun actually cleared the horizon enough to be round, gears grinding angrily as it moved.

Like yesterday, the oncoming sound had convinced him it meant trouble, especially because trucks like that usually meant British Army.

Nobody in Cairo should know enough to actually *arrest* him.

Probably.

So he'd staggered out into the morning sun, thankfully looking west at the flatbed as four crazy Egyptians in robes started unloading boxes and what apparently were empty fuel barrels, rolling them noisily across the packed dirt.

"*Efendim*," the first one said politely as he got close.

Finn just stared at the man blankly, until it become obvious that he intended to put the various barrels inside *Cerberus*. Finn started counting when he realized that one of them had blue paint on the outside, and the other seven were red. Around here, that usually meant gasoline.

"Hans," Finn yelled, hoping his partner in crime was within earshot.

The rear hatch of the plane opened up and Hans handed the closest man a seat that had been disconnected from the floor and folded up.

"She did say early today," Hans just grinned at him as Finn stood there, almost numb.

"It's Cairo," Finn said. "I thought that meant by noon or something."

"Did she look like a woman who waits until noon?" the big German asked with a laugh.

"Well, crap," Finn said.

"I have this covered," Hans said. "You go shower and shave. We'll get her to take us someplace nice for breakfast and then figure things out, okay?"

Finn wanted to argue the point, but he could see that black monster in the middle distance, coming up the road to the airstrip, so he set out, grabbing his Dopp kit and a spare shirt that looked clean to go shave and tidy up.

Behind him, he could hear Hans getting the workers sorted out, removing most of the seats from the back to free up weight and cargo space. That was going to be critical, if they had to haul that much fuel and water. He was looking at *Cerberus* being right at flight capacity, even removing most of the seats. He could do it, but they might need to wait until early morning tomorrow to take off when the air was heaviest, because *Cerberus* would be a lumbering beast to get aloft.

Burn that bridge when he got there.

There was a latrine that the Brits had put in at some point. Cinder block walls and a concrete floor with drains. Someone had even put in a well and a tank on the roof, so there was water for showers. Lukewarm, but better than back home if you were in too much of a hurry to boil some.

Not living in a trench, in all that mud, was one of the prime reasons Finn had worked so hard to get into the pilot training program, even if he had ended up in a spotter plane, rather than up dogfighting with the crazy ones.

He'd also come back from the war alive, unlike many others up in the sky.

Finn showered quickly and took his time shaving, aware that he would probably have two pretty women to deal with today, even if they were both far too young to be interested in an old fart like him.

Ghada wasn't that bad, he supposed, since twenty-eight made her only twelve years younger, but Miss Shirazi was young enough to be his daughter, depending.

A little aftershave today, just in case. A nice shirt.

He almost looked like a professional. Hopefully he'd be able to fool the women.

Hans already knew better.

Still, Finn ambled back down the length of the airstrip with a jaunt in his step and a gorgeous view of things.

The fuel truck had come along while he was gone and started to top off *Cerberus*'s tanks. After that, they would be at it a while, filling up the barrels. Assuming all went well on the way there, they'd be able to fly someplace flat enough, put down, and refill the tanks with a hand pump before flying on to the destination.

With a good wind, *Cerberus* could haul everything safely probably six hundred miles, but she'd just said out in the desert somewhere, cryptically not giving him a course or a distance, other than to point out that he could make it.

If she was serious, they needed to have a conversation that might not be as polite and pleasant as someone who just wanted to run down to Aswan or maybe back to Rome.

The two women were standing near Hans as Finn got closer. The Egyptian men were obviously just workers, but they were also far more obsequious and polite around Miss Shirazi than Finn'd ever seen from local boys.

That either meant she had more money than he thought, which was possible, or she was related to somebody these men feared.

Food for thought.

He nodded to the women as he walked up.

"How close are we going to be on weight?" he asked the big Kraut.

Hans had a clipboard and a pencil already, noting every-thing and doing sums. Again, exactly why he was such a great mechanic.

Or Loadmaster, in this case.

"Take off into the wind, pretty much right at dawn," Hans replied after a moment. "We'll be right at maximum takeoff weight, and the heat of the day will sneak up on us pretty hard."

Finn yelled in Egyptian at the guy on the truck manning the hand pump, and got back a rough estimate of another hour to finish filling. *Cerberus* hadn't been dry, but they were still going to need to pump something like six hundred gallons of fuel this morning. If they had a powered pump, that might go pretty quick, but Finn assumed the boys would be taking turns for a while.

Hopefully the little lady was paying them nice.

Or they were that afraid of her.

"Mr. Severijns," Miss Shirazi said with a nod as he turned to her. "Hans was explaining that you would probably need the rest of the day to pack things away properly, and that the heat possibly already precluded takeoff."

"And you still haven't told us where we're going," he added. "I can fly us down to Aswan and across, or southwest to the Kharga Oasis, where we should be able to refuel and then we're good to get home. Which direction is closer to wherever the hell you want to go?"

He didn't have any problems with smart, pretty, rich girls. Especially not formal businesswomen who didn't look like they needed a knight in shining armor to come save them, but him being treated as a junior varsity walk-on really wasn't going to make him smile.

And her accent kept throwing him sideways, since she sounded so posh and yet looked more like a local.

"How good are you on your geography, Mr. Severijns?" she asked.

"Call me Finn," he said. "My father is Mr. Severijns and he owns the general store at Seaver's Corner, back in Montana."

"Just so, Finn," she said tartly. "We'll be going south of the Black Desert and up onto the Gilf Kebir, out onto the western edge, at a place called Gabal El Uweinat."

It really didn't help that she sounded like an Egyptian when she said those words, but Finn was lost anyway.

Hans nodded and began asking her questions, but Finn didn't follow the gist.

"I can tell we'll need to have you read my copy of Ahmed Hassanein Bey's book *The Lost Oases,*" Shirazi said. "He was the one who explored that region in 1923 and found the various petroglyphs, as well as new water sources."

"So you're looking for cave drawings?" Finn asked, still trying to wrap his head around what this woman was up to.

"No, Mr.—Finn," she said. "But I'd rather not try to describe it until we actually get there and I can test my theories."

"Fine," he said after a moment, realizing that she might be even more stubborn than he was, miracle that might be. "You mentioned tribesmen yesterday."

"The Senussi Brotherhood, yes," she said. "They should be well to the west, in Libyan territory. As I understand it, right now they drive their cattle up into one of the valleys, block off the entrance with stones, and leave the creatures for several months before returning. We should not encounter them at present."

"We'll be needing weapons anyway," Finn stuck his jaw out. "Wilderness like that, you're likely to encounter all manner of trouble."

"Can you acquire what you need today?" she asked. "I really would like to depart first thing tomorrow, if possible."

"Hans?" he turned to his partner.

"Jubal?" Hans asked. "Or maybe Magdy?"

"I'd rather Jubal, if we had a choice," Finn said.

"I'll handle it," the big Kraut said. "English or German?"

"Makes me no difference," Finn shrugged. ".303's an easier kick. 8mm has longer range. Prefer a box magazine to a stripper clip, if it is an option."

He turned back to the woman. Women. Dangerous creatures.

"Food?" he asked. "See that we should have enough water already."

"British Army rations," Miss Shirazi smiled up at him. "One box, so enough for all of us for a fortnight, if necessary. Plus Ghada and I will also have weapons. And Ghada might be a better shot than either of you."

"I'll rely on the two of you to save my bacon, then," Finn smiled frostily at the two women.

He wasn't one of those city boys who presumed girls were meek and helpless creatures, although Miss Shirazi didn't look like she'd ever butchered a hog. Ghada had a knife on her belt with a curve like a waning moon, and Finn was willing to bet that she'd killed more than her share of pigs.

Except she was Muslim. Goats, then. Smaller than pigs. Just as mean.

"So what should we do next, Finn?" Shirazi asked.

"I'll watch the workers," Hans said. "If you see Jubal in town, let him know what we need, or send him out?"

"Will do," Finn said simply. "Now, ladies, I think you should take me out to a nice breakfast in town. I'll need to arrange a few things and get them delivered back here later, and I can walk home after that, while you go find that book I should read. Then I guess you'll need to be here before first light, so we can depart on time."

"Excellent," she said, turning and heading towards the vehicle, Ghada trailing.

She stopped after a few steps and turned to look at him.

"Coming, Finn?" she asked brightly.

Finn nodded and wondered just how much trouble he'd gotten himself into this time.

CHAPTER FIVE

Brunch had gone well. Better than Zareen had expected. For an American, Finn had apparently spent enough time in Europe to acquire far better manners than perhaps she had been expecting of a simple pilot from Montana.

Ghada had chosen to wait in the car rather than join them, so Zareen had been alone with Finn, settling for a croissant and some thick, bitter coffee while the man went with something that approximated the standard American breakfast he had probably known as a youngster. Eggs. Sausages. Toast. Some greens on the side. Potatoes.

More food than she would eat in two days, but the man easily weighed double what she did, much of it muscle.

They were outside the café now, walking into one of the areas where Zareen would not have ventured alone. Even Ghada at her side might not have been sufficient to ward off unwelcome advances and thieves, but Finn had the most magnificent scowl on his face as he walked. It was almost like how various monsters in movies were held at bay by a person showing them a crucifix, to watch the locals shy away from the big American.

Better, he was treating her like his employer, walking on her immediate left without an expectation that he should offer an elbow for her to hold, with Ghada a few paces back.

Cairo had been trying, at times. Perhaps what she needed was a permanent employee like Finn Severijns to cause troublemakers to rethink their options.

They were at the mouth of yet another alley that exuded a stench of rot and decay, like a dragon of pestilence breathing out. Zareen regretted not having her Mauser with her this morning, but she had Ghada. And Finn, she supposed.

Still, perhaps next time she would affect a more piratical motif, with her pistol on one hip and a fencing saber on the other, just to keep the locals from eyeing her with such unmasked resentment and predatory interest.

She supposed that they saw her as an Egyptian woman waiting on a foreigner, when Finn spoke Arabic as well as she did. He might even speak the local Egyptian dialect better, from what she'd heard him say.

Zareen supposed that she could say something to Finn, just so the men and women around her would hear an English accent, but that just sounded like inviting trouble.

Finn had walked to the mouth of the alley and knelt down in front of a beggar. An ancient in tattered robes with a scraggly beard. She heard a coin rattle into the man's cup.

Words were murmured back and forth, but she wasn't close enough to catch more than the sound, watching the vicinity lest someone draw too close.

Finn rose abruptly and nodded to her, turning and backtracking with a long stride she had to stretch to keep up with.

"Good news?" Zareen asked as she caught up with the man.

"Maybe," he said, slowing as he remembered he had company. "Have a lead on Jubal. You're sure you want to tag along? We're going some rough places."

Zareen fixed the man with a hard gaze, almost daring him to say something harsh.

"Your funeral," he shrugged.

They crossed several blocks into an area that was indeed poorer and more hardscrabble than they had been in earlier. She would have called the place where the beggar was terrible, but she supposed that people like her never made it this far into the maze of streets.

Most outsiders would probably have gotten lost by now, but she had a head for navigation and Ghada didn't know what *lost* was.

She was surprised that Finn could find his way. Nothing anyone had told her earlier about the man had suggested this deep of a familiarity with Cairo's slums.

She made a mental note to inquire sometime, once they had returned to brighter quarters.

Finn stopped in the middle of a street, Zareen might have more charitably called a wide alley, but for the shop fronts and buildings of flats facing them from all sides.

He surprised her by turning to Ghada now, a look of focused intent on his otherwise pleasant features.

"Rough joint," he said simply. "Likely trouble, but you're safer indoors than waiting out here. Questions?"

"Should I kill someone causing me offense?" Ghada asked in a tone that Zareen was expecting to sound mocking but came out deadly serious.

"Only if they pull a weapon," Finn said.

He nodded in her direction, smiled briefly, and then walked towards an open doorway on the left.

It was an old building, worn and showing its age in the way the walls had settled at different angles, leaving cracks in the old plaster that needed to be redone.

Or perhaps the owners were waiting for the walls themselves to just collapse, so something new could be erected in its place.

Round tables set around a small room, with the shutters open to provide light and whatever breeze got lost enough to find its way in there.

Hookahs in two corners were surrounded by several men each, passing the pipe around and horizontal in various states of decay.

Zareen didn't smell tobacco smoke in the air. It was a different smell, one she had read about, but never smelled.

So, an opium den? Interesting.

Not a place she had ever been, but she had studied them enough to see the similarities to the Oriental versions.

Big men in various spots along the walls looked like bouncers, house ruffians hired to keep the customers from causing trouble, or helping to drag bodies off to a corner when they had had enough.

Finn ignored the mass of humanity and walked to a table in the back, left corner, almost in shadows and lit by a candle in a translucent red vase. Zareen followed, grateful that she had Ghada with her, as some of the men studied her with hostile eyes.

Money and power had kept her safe from the depredations of strange men, but the crowd in here didn't look like they would care all that much. She definitely needed to bring the Mauser with her after this. And perhaps the saber, just to make it a cogent point.

A man awaited them at the table. He was dressed in the Western style, with a brown suit and tie and black hair that had been slicked back, but the man was Egyptian. Reedy, almost to the point of emaciated. She might have suggested jaundiced, even, but he didn't have the yellow tinge to his skin.

Just the bags under his eyes.

He watched them now like a falcon that had just had its hood removed. Aware. Predatory. Hungry.

But only for a moment, before his face cleared into a pleasant neutrality when he saw her.

Zareen wondered what thoughts went through the man's mind. She didn't know him on sight, but supposed that he might know who she was.

After all, there weren't many Anglo-Persian nobles like her in Cairo right now.

"Please, sit," he said, gesturing to the three empty chairs before him.

Finn did sit, so Zareen joined him a moment later. Ghada moved to the side with her back to the wall, where she could watch both Jubal, assuming that was who this man was, and the other ruffians about the place.

"Good morning, Jubal," Finn confirmed in a bright, serious tone. "Hans and I are headed out to the western deserts and need to pick up some weapons. The Italians never would let me carry anything big on *Cerberus,* so we'd like to acquire two or three matching rifles, ammunition, and cleaning kits."

Zareen glanced over at the American, wondering if he expected her to pay for such a purchase, but he'd mentioned nothing of the sort earlier. Plus, he had negotiated a pretty good deal for himself, with some upfront money already changing hands. Perhaps he was investing that cash now?

Jubal studied them both for a long moment.

"Will you be returning to Cairo afterwards?" he asked in an off-hand way that had Zareen confused.

Where else would they go?

"Indeed," Finn nodded. "So preferably nothing easily traced. And either English or German. None of that Italian crap. Nor those weird Japanese rifles you picked up somewhere."

"They were quality equipment," Jubal's smile finally emerged.

"Nobody carries any ammunition for them except what you might import," Finn laughed. ".303 or 8mm is almost as common as fleas around here."

Jubal nodded in a placating way, laughter evident in his eyes.

Zareen wondered how many people the man might have enticed to buy his Japanese armaments, just to then be unfortunately stuck with also getting ammunition from him afterwards. It would make a profitable venture, as they were either locked in to purchasing more, or had to turn around later and buy other weapons, possibly trading the Imperial Japanese weapons back in for some credit. Rifles that could then be resold to the next victim.

"How quickly were you departing?" Jubal asked.

"How quickly can you deliver them out to the airstrip?" Finn countered, not telling the man anything.

Zareen approved of Finn's subtlety. Poker and treaty negotiations, but perhaps also illicit arms deals. She would need to remember to tell Father that when she was next in Scotland.

"I have some Enfield Mark IVs," the man said after a moment. "Newly shipped and intended for Abyssinia, but they seem to have fallen off a truck somewhere and been lost."

"Abyssinia?" Finn asked.

Jubal shrugged.

"The English cannot complain about such weapons without admitting where they came from in the first place," he said, smiling like a shark now. "Everyone just sort of looks the other way and pretends nothing happened. New, still packed in grease. Four of them, if you'd like to handle the initial cleaning yourself."

Zareen watched as Finn did the maths in his head, with little gestures and wiggles, almost like he was dancing to some tune only he could hear. She barely kept from grinning at the image.

"How much?" he finally asked.

Jubal quoted a price that sounded low to Zareen, but she wasn't in the smuggling business. And didn't suppose, after a moment of thought, that Jubal had paid all that much for them.

Or perhaps he wanted them off his hands before someone came along and asked questions.

Just how deep into the criminal underworld was this quest going to take her?

The two men dickered, but it was a friendly thing. Hardly any profanities exchanged, and voices that never rose above what one might hear in a polite salon. You might have thought they were discussing the price of tea imports, rather than working out a deal for illegal armaments stolen from a British Army base, possibly in broad daylight.

"You'll have a car swing by later and drop them off?" Finn asked as they agreed to a price.

Jubal nodded and Zareen watched the American pull several pound notes from his pocket and count them for the Egyptian, sliding them across the table where they disappeared into a pocket quickly.

"Pleasure doing business with you," Finn said as he rose suddenly.

"And you, old friend," Jubal replied. "Perhaps there will be more business we might undertake when you get back from wherever you are headed."

"Perhaps," Finn nodded.

He drew her and Ghada into his wake, stepping smartly around one of the bouncers removing a customer to what Zareen presumed was a mat in back to sleep off whatever it was he had done.

Outside, she caught his sleeve after they had gotten a block or so back in the direction they had originally come.

"So you just gave the man money, and he'll deliver?" she asked, a little surprised.

Weren't illicit arms deals supposed to be seedy, dangerous things?

"He has a reputation to uphold," Finn nodded sagely. "And I assume the weapons were reported stolen, or will be at some point. Once we take delivery, we'll clean two of them, and then find a box to store the other two. At that point, someone has to have a good reason to want to inspect them. We'll deal with it then."

"You are not afraid of being arrested?" Zareen pressed.

"Won't be the first time," Finn shrugged, glancing back

up the street at the traffic around them. "Or the last, more likely than not."

He started to walk again, and Zareen fell in beside him.

Hopefully, she had made a wise choice in Finn Severijns. People who were supposed to know such things had suggested him as the best option available on the market, and he was treating them well.

However, he was also introducing her to a much different part of Cairo than she had been viscerally aware of.

At some point, though, he was going to start asking questions.

CHAPTER SIX

A knock at the door caused Didier to look up from his newspaper and draw a pistol from his blazer pocket. It was a petite thing, almost harmless looking, practically engulfed in his meaty fist, but far more dangerous than it would appear at first glance. Didier had specifically designed it that way.

"Who is it?" he called, aiming the weapon at the door, in case he needed to kill someone through the thick wood.

Hopefully, nobody was home across the hall who would be at risk of a small rocket blasting through their room if he fired.

"Bertrand," a muffled voice carried.

Didier rose, putting out his nearly spent cigarette in the tray on the table as he did. Moving to the door, he unlocked the bolt and opened it.

The man in the hallway had a cruel face. Anger and violence never seemed far from the surface. Like Didier, he wore a plain suit, brown and light for the desert heat. Bertrand's was looser, designed to obscure pistols, knives, and dynamite packs, as needed.

Not everyone wanted to share their scientific discoveries with their competition, but everyone could be bought, beaten, or simply killed to get them out of the way.

Didier stepped to one side and Bertrand slipped into the room like a ghost. Or an assassin. Which he also was.

Didier closed the door and set the bolt again before returning the pistol to his pocket.

"What news?" he asked, returning to the table and grabbing his packet of cigarettes.

He hated smoking the cheap Turkish blends they had in Cairo, but nobody carried French cigarettes for anything less than a king's ransom.

"The woman is moving," his assistant replied, taking a seat on the bed.

Didier would have preferred a proper flat, or even an office of some sort, but the Englishwoman had never stayed in place long enough for Didier to set up a professional shop.

Just one anonymous hotel room after another, tracking this madwoman across countries and continents.

"How soon?" Didier asked.

"We almost missed her," Bertrand said, his face drawn. "She has hired an American pilot and craft, but they needed today to make arrangements. I expect her to depart in the morning."

Didier felt a jolt of excitement course through his entire being.

So close now? Had she found something? A hint? A clue? Proof of extraterrestrials meddling in human affairs?

Didier didn't care if Martians were truly here or merely visiting. If they had not revealed themselves yet, they were either afraid of humans, or loathed them so greatly that they would not interfere.

That meant that he had time for his various plans to unfold, but not if the woman had found something and he couldn't subsequently obtain it.

France's Third Republic was doomed. Democracy itself was a failed experiment. Germany and Italy were rearming and showing the world the strength of fascism to get things done. Another war was on the near horizon, one that would see the decadent republics erased. And none of the silliness of bringing back the even-more-degenerate, inbred aristocrats who thought to restore some foolish former glory.

No, rule by strength. By power.

By Might, itself.

Didier Beauchêne would have the secrets of the aliens so he could make even greater weapons. Armageddon was coming, for the very soul of humanity. Didier didn't much care about the racialist fantasies of Hitler or the others. They would respect strength, something the Third Republic had frittered away for a generation. The Poles were the only people he could think of even less prepared to fight a conflagration that would make the previous Great War look like an argument between two chickens in the yard.

Fascist France would take her place beside the others, and dictate terms to everyone else, including those damnable Americans.

First, though, he had to have that woman's secrets.

"Do we know where she is going?" Didier leaned forward as he lit another cigarette, drawing a heavy lungful of rich smoke down into the center of his soul.

"Rumors and speculation," Bertrand said, leaning back.

"Tell me," Didier commanded.

"Gilf Kebir seems to be the strongest rumor known," Bertrand replied. "The Western Desert nearly to the Sudan."

"What would she...?" Didier started to ask, but then he stopped and reconsidered.

There had been many potential sightings of alien vessels coming to Earth. Tunguska in 1908. Many people claimed that an alien vessel must have exploded in flight, since no crater was ever found when people looked.

Or the 1930 Curuçá River Event in Brazil, steadily covered up by those tight-lipped bastards at the Vatican.

Meteors impacting the Earth left tremendous scars. There were few on this planet, but one only had to look at the moon overhead to see.

Had Hassanein seen something in 1923? Bedouins had been traversing that desert for thousands of years, but only in the last generation had scientists joined them to explore and map things. And Hassanein had found evidence that the area had once been a great grasslands, with ancient pictographs of wild animals from much farther south carved into the rocks. Perhaps ten thousand years ago, it had been savanna.

Had the man found other things that were being suppressed? Impossible. The Egyptian government held secrets like sand held water.

However, the English would never let go of their stranglehold on all of Egypt, when all they really needed was the Nile Valley and the Suez Canal.

Was there something in the Gilf Kebir that nobody had talked about before now?

"Do you know where she's staying?" Didier asked, putting aside all the other questions he had until he could find out more.

Perhaps he needed to reread Hassanein's explorations? Or simply steal or at least copy whatever notes and maps the woman had.

"The Hotel International," the assassin replied. "She has a suite for at least another month, suggesting that she will be returning here."

"You will need to break in tonight, after she has gone to bed, to read her journal or notes," Didier decided. "We must find out where she is going, if we can."

"Kill her?" the man brightened up.

"No, we don't know what clues she is pursuing now," Didier said. "And if she is planning to return to Cairo, we can always steal whatever she finds then. Or kidnap her and convince her to tell us what she knows."

He paused, reviewing his options as Bertrand watched.

"Who is the pilot?" he asked.

"An American named Severijns," the killer sneered. "Was employed by the Italians to run passengers and mail. Kept the plane when their business failed."

"Is he a threat?" Didier studied his assassin.

"Only to the woman's virginity," Bertrand laughed roughly. "His German mechanic might be a problem, but I can always shoot them both."

"Again, not until we know exactly what her plans are," Didier said, crushing out his cigarette as he got down to his fingers. "We are not prepared to chase her into and across the desert, but we can prepare a trap for her when she returns. Find out what she has written down, and do not be seen."

"As you command." Bertrand rose and made his way to the door.

Didier followed and locked it again when the man was gone.

What had Zareen Shirazi found? For so long, she had been pursuing leads in Spain and Portugal. It made no sense to suddenly pivot and race madly the entire length of the

Mediterranean Sea to set up shop in Cairo unless she had discovered something.

He had to know.

The future of the world might hinge on it.

CHAPTER SEVEN

Zareen usually slept lightly. The heat of the Cairo night made it even worse, as she had left the windows open to draw in any breeze, however light, to try to stir the air in here.

On her nightstand, a small travel clock slowly ticked to itself, the radium hands only now approaching midnight. She had gone to bed early, tossing fitfully as she tried to fall asleep, since she had to be up several hours before dawn in order to prepare, and then have her new driver deliver her to the airstrip.

Finn had been adamant that they needed to depart just as the sun was cresting the horizon, to take maximum advantage of the heavy coolness of the air to take off and the first light to see. *Cerberus* would be at rather close to maximum takeoff weight with the load, which she had not foreseen in her planning.

Zareen had been dreaming. Something light and fanciful, unfit for the harsh realities of daylight in the world of a woman split halfway between English racists who didn't care for her Persian blood, and Persian nobles who viewed any outsiders as beneath them.

At least she had inherited stubbornness from both her parents.

She wasn't sure what it was that woke her.

Something was wrong.

This was Cairo and she slept with the windows open at night, so she carefully slipped a hand under her pillow to find the comfortable weight of the Mauser. She wrapped her hand around the round, wooden grip and opened her eyes just enough to see the room on the left side of the bed that she was facing.

Nothing but wall, but she was facing away from the window.

She listened.

No sound but those of a city at night, where even the vehicles were at a distance, lest the noise disturb the wealthy who could afford such a hotel.

Zareen considered her options. She slept in a linen shift under a light enough blanket, with the heavier one at the foot of the bed that she might pull up later if she felt a chill.

Rather than sit up, she slid over the rest of the way and silently dropped off the edge of the bed, into the corner away from the window, drawing the black Mauser with her.

One thumb up to draw back the long hammer. Then drop the safety block clear of the firing pin.

Only her eyes and the pencil-like tip of the barrel appeared as she scanned the rest of her small bedroom.

She had taken one of the fanciest suites at the hotel, itself among the most posh and advanced in Cairo. She even had a bathroom off to one side, with a toilet and a shower/tub.

Such decadence, but there was something utterly sublime

about relaxing in a pool of cool water after a hot day, scrubbing off a layer of grime and salty dirt, emerging refreshed.

The door was closed, as she had left it earlier. No light appeared under the panel.

Zareen rose on bare feet and padded carefully across the carpeted floor. Again, decadence, not to have old hardwoods polished by age.

There. A light from the main room.

Not a lamp or the overhead. It came and went, flashing and disappearing.

A pocket flash?

Yes, quite possibly.

Zareen scowled, envisioning some worthless thief sneaking into her suite to rifle her things.

She closed her left hand on the cool brass handle of the door to the main room and turned it as slowly as she could.

Pulling ever so slightly, she opened it a crack that she could press an eye against.

Indeed, a pocketflash of some sort, in the hands of a tall, skinny man.

He was dressed as a Westerner, with slacks and a blazer covering his frame and a beaver fedora obscuring his features.

The intruder stood at her writing desk, located near the window with a grand view of the river itself in the near distance, where she might sit and compose letters or poetry, if she were a different kind of woman.

He seemed to be reading her papers, the cheek of the bastard.

Zareen opened the door farther, so outraged now that she didn't bother returning for the dressing gown draped over the chair behind her.

"What's going on?" she demanded, reaching out and flipping the switch by the door that illuminated the lamp on the very writing desk this trespasser had violated.

The man glanced over his shoulder in something approximating surprise and fumbled in his jacket.

Zareen had taken half a step forward when something flashed towards her and she stumbled to one side. Father had taught her to shoot his old Mauser, so she didn't accidentally fire a shot into the ceiling, but her brain had registered the motion and thrown her from harm's way.

The knife embedded itself into the doorframe with a solid thunk like a jack chopping lumber.

The stranger had moved, so she set her feet and raised the Mauser again. But instead of rushing her, he raced across the room to the balcony door, itself ajar.

Zareen fired at him. One shot at the black ghost as he moved almost impossibly fast and agile. The sound was like Joshua's Horn bringing down the walls of Jericho in the small space.

And then he was gone.

Zareen was appalled. She was on the fourth floor and the man had gone right over the balcony itself into darkness.

Regardless of propriety in her nearly nude state, she raced to the balcony as well. Behind her, a door opened. Ghada was awake and joining her.

The outside of the hotel was only vaguely lit, so it was hard to make him out, but the stranger was moving like a spider now, two floors down and three balconies across.

She considered shooting at him again, but he looked at her as she aimed.

Then he let go of the railing, plummeting out of sight before she could react.

He was only on the first floor at that point. A mere ten or

so feet to drop, and she seemed to remember bushes of some sort near that corner, so he must have been prepared for something soft to break his fall.

Darkness, though, so she could not fire again, without the risk of hitting an innocent bystander.

Ghada was a warmth at her side when she glanced over, crescent knives in each hand as she normally practiced in the early morning.

"What was it?" her bodyguard asked.

"A man was in the suite," Zareen answered. "Reading my journal, I think."

She turned now, setting the safety on the dangerous pistol and walking over to her desk.

Indeed, he had been reading her notebook. Lisbon, from the page that was open when she got there.

All of her important papers were in the hotel vault. Passport, most of her money, things like that. He hadn't even bothered with the hundred or so pounds that were in an envelope tucked into her book.

"A thief, perhaps?" Zareen asked.

She looked up when she realized that Ghada wasn't close by.

Instead, the woman was standing at the door to Zareen's bedroom, pulling the knife from the frame where the man's throw had embedded it.

Quite deep, from the way the woman had to saw at the thing to withdraw it.

Zareen joined her. Heard the woman curse under her breath as she got a closer look at it.

"Our friends have made it to Cairo," Ghada said quietly, holding the weapon out.

Zareen examined the weapon, nearly a foot long with

both edges sharp. The pommel was black and wrapped in a thin, leather cord.

It was the crossguard that marked the weapon.

An eagle, with an olive wreath in its claws. Inside the loop of leaves was an upright fist.

"Beauchêne," she growled as she took it.

"One of his killers, most likely," Ghada said.

Zareen agreed. The man had many, the way a dead carcass by the side of the road had flies.

A knock at the door to the suite drew her eyes up from the weapon.

"Madam Shirazi, are you well?" a man's voice called.

Presumably, the night manager had been called when a gunshot woke other guests.

"Yes," she yelled back. "A minute."

She handed the blade back to Ghada.

"Hide this for now," she commanded the woman. "The intruder was an unknown thief and I chased him off. Nothing more."

Rather than do anything else, Zareen returned to her bedroom long enough to grab the dressing gown and belt it about herself.

It was still a scandalous way to open the door, especially to a man in the dead of night, but she would need to deflect the manager as she lied to him about what really happened.

Otherwise, there would possibly be police, as well, and she could not allow that, or she would never make her meeting with *Cerberus*. It was becoming critical that she not be delayed in Cairo at this point, especially if Beauchêne had indeed followed her thus far.

She dared not risk letting that man get to Gilf Kebir ahead of her.

At least she had not written the important clues down.

Zareen kept the Mauser in her hand and pasted a smile on her face as she opened the door.

This would be a performance worthy of the ages.

CHAPTER EIGHT

Crap, they hadn't even waited for the first false dawn to arrive this time, had they?

Finn had slept in his hammock again that night. It was better than waking up to things crawling over him in the night, or wriggling up next to him for warmth.

It also kept him in a good spot to see people coming and going.

Not that he expected to have to deal with thieves trying to steal things off *Cerberus*, but right now that represented pretty much everything he owned, not counting all the seats he and Hans had managed to talk the Brits into letting him store in their hangar until he got back.

There was a truck coming up the road to the airstrip, driven by someone who really didn't like the gear shifter on the thing.

Finn hadn't really been sleeping so much as dozing. Most nights, he really only needed about six hours of sleep, and if he could nap during the day, even less.

Hans got grumpy if he didn't get eight or more hours of

beauty sleep. Not that it had worked to date, but there was always hope there.

Finn didn't recognize the truck. Didn't look like British or Egyptian Army. Looked like an old Ford with a flatbed and stakes. Dead black, like they were. Blackout headlights on the front. Needed a tune-up pretty bad, even for an old Ford.

He'd have thought those things were tough. Old Henry must not have expected desert sand and grit.

Finn checked his watch. Wound it while he was thinking about it, just to make sure it was good, in case the next hour turned into some sort of circus and he wanted accurate time.

Still three hours until dawn.

Couldn't be Shirazi and her sidekick this early, could it?

He reached down and untangled his boots from each other, checking to make sure nothing was asleep in them before he climbed out of his hammock and slid his feet home. Heavy boots that were necessary any time you had to walk in rough terrain. Maybe them old fancy cavalry boys liked knee-high slip-ons. Or the cowboys back home, but Finn wasn't a rider. He preferred a wide steel cup protecting his toes and a heavy tread keeping nails at bay.

And ankle high was good enough for most snakes and scorpions.

Sure enough, that truck was coming towards him. Nobody else down here to talk to once they went past the last of the hangars.

Finn had acquired an old Government issue M1911 Colt after the war. They had been damned near everywhere at that point, and bloody cheap. Everyone in Europe these days was either still using 9mm for a service cartridge, or something even smaller, like the 7.63mm Mauser that was older than he was.

He preferred the old-fashioned kick of a .45 ACP. If he had to shoot something, Finn didn't want it getting back up again afterwards, which was a risk with the smaller calibers.

He normally kept it out of sight up in the cockpit, tucked along the outer wall next to his left knee where he could reach it if he needed but passengers wouldn't see.

After the last few days, he'd taken to sleeping with it in a shoulder holster. Not exactly comfortable, but worth the potential drawbacks.

Like being unarmed as a strange truck raced up at him in the middle of the night, outside of Cairo, where the laws weren't always as strictly enforced as they would be in Boston. When Boston enforced them.

Finn reached up and unsnapped the holster now, drawing the big iron brute out and holding it down by his side. Hammer was back and the safety was set, just like he'd been taught, a lifetime ago it seemed these days.

Wouldn't necessarily do much to someone inside the truck, but he could sure kill the vehicle itself with a quick shot through the radiator. Or shoot out a tire if they got too close.

Headlights found him finally and the driver jammed hard on the brakes, screeching the truck to a halt. The engine stalled as he did so.

Finn didn't figure he looked all that friendly right now, standing like a cowboy in the middle of the street for a shootout showdown. All he really needed was a hat, but those were a pain in the ass inside a cockpit, so he'd never bothered.

After a moment, the driver started the engine up and put

the vehicle back in gear, oozing sedately forward this time and turning to their left a little, so Finn wasn't staring at the angry dragon's eyes of the headlights.

It coasted to a stop about twenty yards away and this time the driver shut the engine down completely.

There was a moon just waxing past half-full, and a few lights around, so Finn could see the door open and Ghada got out.

He realized that he had no idea what the woman's last name was, as she'd only ever had a first name. Felt wrong, now that he thought about it, but Brits and Egyptians had strange opinions on propriety, and it wasn't his place to try and fix them.

Miss Shirazi emerged a moment later, dressed for a day on the desert rather than a salon, in that same outfit she'd worn the first time he'd met her. Or close enough.

Driver emerged as well, a mite more tentative than the women, but Finn hadn't put his pistol away, either.

You never knew.

She said something and the driver suddenly raced around to the back of the truck, noisily pulling the gate to one side and lifting.

Finn began to walk towards them, as the women hadn't approached any closer to where he was.

Driver was an Egyptian fellow. Dressed in pants, shirt, tie, and jacket, rather than robes. No hat. Busy pulling a small chest down from the back of the truck.

Nice trunk. Well made with shiny brass fittings on the corners, rather than something Finn might own. Way too nice.

Heavy, too, from the grunt as the man got it down.

"Good evening, Mr. Severijns," Shirazi said as he got

close. "I hope we aren't too early, but I found it appropriate to depart the hotel post-haste."

He studied her face as he got close, but she wasn't giving anything away.

"Everything okay?" he asked, aware that she had a holster on her right side with a Broomhandle Mauser in it. Hadn't had that yesterday. Or the day before.

Ghada had a hand on the pommel of one of those knives she always kept in her belt.

Neither woman replied.

Must have been one hell of a party.

"*Efendim*," the man with the trunk said as he started to waddle past with that trunk in both hands.

"Put it next to the plane," Finn ordered the tiny man. "We'll load it ourselves in order to balance things correctly."

He looked around, but they were alone in every direction as far as he could see. Even the camels over by the wadi were asleep right now, but they'd sleep through anything except gunfire. Maybe that, too.

Finn followed the man, supervising for lack of anything else useful to be doing right now.

After a moment, he slipped the Colt back into his holster and decided maybe he would look better that way. Less threatening, at least.

Back home, the gun would just disappear under a jacket and be fine. He'd known a few folks like that from before. They were generally bootleggers in those days, but not all that booze had arrived in the trunk of a car.

Finn stepped to one side as the women walked closer. Miss Shirazi slipped a coin to the man, got a tip of an invisible cap, and the fellow scampered off to his truck again.

Engine turned over pretty quickly and the man mashed gears getting turned around and gone.

Finn found himself standing next to Shirazi, with a silent Ghada somewhere off on the far side.

"Someone broke into my room, earlier this evening," she finally said. Her voice had a controlled rage to it that wasn't anything like a helpless damsel in distress. Of course, those sorts of women didn't carry Broomhandles around, either.

Dangerous weapon. Required some training to use right.

Finn would have outwaited her, but he was like that.

For now, he just glanced over and grunted noncommittally. Easier to deal that way when a woman wanted to talk.

"I chased him off," she continued. "Might have even wounded him, but not enough to stop him from climbing down my balcony and we didn't find any blood when we looked, so the shot probably went wide. Still, it suggested that someone in Cairo was concerned enough about what I was doing to try to disrupt my plans, Mister Severijns."

"Finn," he corrected her automatically.

"Finn," she nodded. "Rather than wait, I packed up what goods I needed, stored the rest at the hotel, and had the night manager's assistant drive me out here. I hope that's not an imposition."

Finn checked his watch again.

"Sun's not up for another two and a half hours," he said simply. "Not enough light until false dawn to even try taking off. Who's after you?"

Finn liked the way her eyes got squinty. Made her appear older than the twenty she normally looked.

He smiled and changed tacks, like a good sailboat running into the wind.

"Will whoever it is be a risk here?" he asked. "Should we post guard, shoot anything that moves, that sort of thing? Or are we only facing troubles out there in the desert when we arrive?"

"I doubt they can outrun us to our destination, Finn," she replied, rather obliquely if he had to say so.

"*Cerberus* really only flies around a hundred miles an hour, Miss Shirazi," he said. "Not outrunning anything else in the air."

"Zareen," she said, confusing him.

Must have made his face look good when she looked. She smiled.

"My name is Zareen Shirazi, Finnley Severijns," she continued. "Call me Zareen, please. And if they follow you in the air, we'll know and can try a different direction. Or just scrub things and start over, possibly on foot."

"How nasty are they?" Finn asked.

Out of the corner of his eye, he saw Hans emerge silently from the plane, rifle slung over his shoulder. They hadn't had a chance to fire them yesterday, but both weapons were clean and they had a box of a hundred rounds, which was fine for desert critters and bandits.

Wasn't like he was preparing for a war out there.

At least he hoped not.

"Bad enough that I'd like to be away from them for now," she said. "We may need to find a different route home, and possibly not even return to Cairo, but instead retire to a different place and have my gear forwarded. We'll worry about that later."

Finn nodded rather than argue. He understood that plans could change. If they really had to, he could make Aswan coming back, rather than going north to Kharga, though from Kharga he could make any number of ports along the Med if he didn't want to land back at Cairo.

He'd let her decide. For now, he was just the hired hand. Still...

"Ya know, if time is critical, there is another option," he offered, willing to kick himself, but hey, he had a lady in need, and his Ma would never let him hear the end of it if she heard.

"Do tell, Finn?" she smiled at him now.

"The Kharga Oasis is about three hundred miles away," he said. "Normally, with a load this heavy, the plan had been to overnight there so we could take off again early. If we left right now, we'd be there not that long after dawn. Depending on the weather and the ground crew, we might get fueled up again in an hour and still have heavy enough air to take off again today."

Finn really didn't like the way her eyes lit up when he said that. Suggested that maybe the trouble brewing was smart enough to follow them to Kharga, and he'd have some sort of issues tonight if he was still there.

Maybe it was better to push now and sleep rough.

"Could you?" she asked brightly, all cheeriness itself.

Oh, what the hell.

"Hans, start packing," Finn yelled. "I'll clean up here and we'll leave in ten minutes."

Hopefully, the ladies had already visited a latrine. He and Hans could always just piss on a handy palm tree once he had the ladies aboard.

God only knew what kind of trouble he'd gotten himself into this time.

CHAPTER NINE

Zareen wondered if she should have brought something to cover her ears against the incredible noise, but even her fingers didn't help. Those three engines generated a sound that she felt in her bones.

She and Ghada were right behind the compact cockpit where the two men sat, Finn on her left and Hans on the right. The dashboard, what she could see of it from the first seats behind them, was a complicated mess. More than anything she had trained on, but she'd also never flown something with more than one engine.

The floor under her feet was raw metal, which surprised her, but Hans had explained when she asked that most of their passengers were military men these days and used to something like that. Plus, not having any carpet or luxuries saved weight, which extended their range.

Anything to save costs, which she appreciated. Those extra miles made it possible for *Cerberus* to transport her to where she needed quickly, and then get back, without having to rely on a caravan of camels and hard men that might not be as reliable as this pair of pilots had a reputation for.

The engines screamed at her like the worst *ban sidhes* from the Scottish mountains coming down onto the moors after her. For several seconds, she wasn't sure that they would even be able to lift off, and would instead have to scrub and wait for dawn, but *Cerberus* itself seemed to understand her need, because the craft made a crouching motion under her feet, and then leapt into the air, driving her heart into her stomach for a second. Out the window by her side, she suddenly saw the nighttime lights of Cairo below as the plane fought for altitude.

And then something broke loose and they were racing into the sky, free.

She dared draw a breath as the sound of the engines backed off quickly, until they were just a low, rumbling growl in the background and she could hear a hiss over everything.

Neither pilot seemed concerned, which surprised her, until Zareen realized that she was hearing the sound of the air itself racing over the skin of the aircraft.

How intriguing.

"Next stop: the Kharga Oasis," Finn said in a voice barely above normal to speak to her. "We're going to push a little to get there early, so hopefully we'll be able to land and find a fueling truck, and not be on the ground that long and can hop up again."

She nodded, rather than speak.

All she had done thus far was delay the conversation she would need to have with Finn and Hans.

The actual coordinates she would have them fly to.

What they said at that point would be interesting.

CHAPTER TEN

"You're just lucky the woman's not a better shot," Didier growled quietly at the man, not daring to raise his voice.

The walls here weren't actually made of paper, but the couple in the next room behind him would probably not appreciate Didier offering color commentary the next time they engaged in marital pursuits just on the other side of this wall.

Bertrand had removed his jacket and was inspecting the sleeve. Didier assumed that it would require a tailor to fix. Probably better to have one replace both sleeves, since Shirazi's bullet had opened up the upper arm like one of Betrand's razor-sharp knives would have done, even as it had missed the skin, however unlikely.

Probably better to just replace it entirely. It wasn't like the tailors here were that expensive, if he only needed to buy a simple blazer.

And the man had gotten Didier what he needed, so he would be willing to buy the man a new jacket.

"I am more concerned about the knife," Bertrand replied, looking up.

"You didn't hurt her, did you?" Didier asked.

"No," Bertrand replied, obviously insulted. "It was meant as a brushback pitch, and it succeeded, but I wasn't expecting the gun in her hand, so I had no chance to recover my blade afterward. So she knows *we* are after her now, and not just some random burglar."

Brushback? Ah, probably a baseball term. Bertrand had spent enough time in America to pick up some unfortunate linguistic habits. And listened to games whenever he could find one on the radio.

"She already knew that," Didier said. "All she has learned is that we're here in Cairo, on her heels, rather than still in Lisbon, sniffing for her trail."

"Perhaps," Bertrand said. "She is looking for the Man With No Face, but all she knows is that he is in Cairo. At least that is all she wrote down in her journal. There was nothing that suggested anything more specific than just Gilf Kebir for her current mission."

"Just as well," Didier said. "If she is not around, then we can begin searching for the Man With No Face ourselves. Perhaps we can solve his present while she seeks his past."

After all, he didn't need much. Just a little advanced, alien technology would probably be sufficient to give him the edge he needed to conquer France. After that, the Fascist Axis would be enough to conquer the world.

CHAPTER ELEVEN

The Man With No Face heard things slowly in the shadows of Cairo, but he had spent nearly two decades here, slowly working his way into the social fabric of the city, and even this neighborhood itself, until he was a fixture as accepted as anyone born here.

That had been his original mission, once. Quiet infiltration to learn more about human social structures. And until someone from home came here openly seeking First Contact, or found out about his mission and came to arrest him, it was just about the only mission he could pursue.

Well, he could always go hide from all humanity. Not that far from Cairo, in the eastern deserts across the canal, there were a number of humans who had forsworn all contact, living in caves and surviving on offerings from others, as well as what they could scavenge from the desert itself.

Since the Mark Seven didn't require even that much, he would be limited only to the fuel in his reactor, which was likely sufficient for perhaps as much as a century, depending on circumstances.

After that, he might have to find a boat to carry him out into the ocean far enough so that no humans ever located him.

Walking there sounded like too much effort, even for an autonomous unit like him.

However, news of the city and the world eventually reached him. In dribs and drabs. Pieces and whispers. Rumors that didn't have any great meaning to travelers like Magdy the Arms Merchant or others.

However, Asher could assemble them into a whole that meant things to him, where no human would be able to gather them into any sort of a coherent whole.

People were seeking him. Actively. Perhaps even understanding that he had a secret worth chasing.

Hopefully not worth killing over, as he was just a watcher.

But humans were illogical creatures at the best of times.

Worse, there seemed to be more than one group chasing after his shadow, to use a poetical term he had learned from a young man who had spent some time in the café a few years ago.

Arabic was such a flowing and lyrical language. It was certainly a shame that the current political circumstances tended to dictate that English, French, and German were so prominent. Italian might finally be rising. Russian was recovering, but the Soviets had turned inward and seemed content to hold their borders against all threats.

Unless the gentleman in Mexico achieved some success with his dreams.

Asher was just sorry that his transport had been

destroyed in Egypt. There were such other interesting places he could have set down.

But without his humanity, perhaps it was better that he lived in a souq in Cairo for the time being.

Not for the first time, he wondered what would happen to human civilization when they discovered him. What would they do when they found that they weren't alone in the universe, one that was so much larger and more complicated than anyone but the scientifiction writers in the United States seemed to dream about?

He would cross that bridge at some point, but the current political developments did not convince him to expose himself to anyone.

Not yet. Perhaps not ever.

Especially not when he was being sought.

Asher thanked the man who had delivered the latest news, watched the man nod, receive a tip, and depart.

His potential foes were perhaps close.

Actively seeking him in Cairo even now, where the process of elimination would eventually lead them to him. And only random chance suggested that he would be the tenth man so sought, so perhaps he should consider exercising his evasion programming now, rather than waiting until the hunters arrived.

Asher rose. He probably surprised Faisal, leaving so much earlier in the day than normal, but it could not be helped. And he could not speak of his misgivings, as the hunters would ask.

Better that nobody knew the truth.

He made sure that his hood covered his turban, protecting the rear of his cranial unit from accidental discovery if a sudden breeze lifted his hood away.

Exiting the café, he picked a direction at random, walking with the deliberation of a man on a specific errand. Over the last decade, he had explored nearly all of Cairo, so it was not possible for him to actually get lost. He never forgot, and the map he carried in his head was probably better than the ones the local or British authorities had.

Should he transcribe that map onto a large piece of paper and anonymously mail it to someone's cartographic office? Asher considered it as he stepped into an alley and crossed, wending his way carefully through some of the junk and organic fluids that had accumulated.

Midway down the alley, a sound. Asher had time to note the noise that a human male approaching at high speed would make, but it took him several moments to process that the figure was coming directly at him.

A loud crack accompanied the man striking him on the cranial unit with a blunt, heavy object.

Asher turned now, using his advanced reflexes to confront the attacker.

He lashed out, catching the weapon in one hand and jerking it out of the stranger's hand before the human could react.

"Your behavior is inappropriate," Asher said in an unpleasant voice he had learned from Faisal dealing with some of the more unsavory characters that occasionally wandered into the café by mistake.

The human's mouth had fallen open in a manner commensurate with shock and disbelief. His eyes had grown slightly distended, compared to a physiological population spectrum of *normal*.

Asher decided that an example was perhaps called for now.

He could not injure a human. His programming was complicated on the topic, but sufficient to protect them from most things.

Instead, he clenched the weapon in one hand and squeezed carefully. It was a rod of wood. Cyprus, perhaps from the color, but too heavy.

American hickory? Interesting.

He flexed his fingers and thumb inside his glove and the piece of wood shattered into two pieces with a satisfactory crack, shearing into two ragged stumps.

"If I see you again, I will hurt you," Asher lied to the human with as much sincerity as he could put behind the words.

Faisal had used such a phrase to drive off more than one person. To accentuate things, Asher handed the human both pieces of his now-broken club.

"Run now, lest I grow angry."

That seemed sufficient. The human fled without his club, leaving Asher in command of the alley, save for a few local beggars who called it home during the heat of the day.

He glanced over, but none chose to speak. One smiled serenely.

Asher took that as a good sign and continued on his way.

CHAPTER TWELVE

Finn had been concerned about all that weight getting off the ground. It would be worse trying to leave Kharga, since the elevation above sea level would factor in as well. But he had a good idea what it would take now, so it could be done.

Longer use of the runway, possibly all of it instead of the much shorter stretch *Cerberus* usually needed to haul half a dozen passengers and gear into the sky.

Landing would be interesting as well, coming in so early, but again, that likely meant that nobody would be getting ready to leave.

He just had to find someone to refuel him quickly.

Finn wasn't sure who was after Zareen, but the fact that she was armed this morning told him stories. There had been nobody visible flying behind him when he turned enough to see, but that didn't mean anything. A radio signal or even a telegram could get there first. Or a more modern plane than the Ford Trimotor, so old that they didn't even make them anymore.

At least the sun was coming up behind them now.

Enough that the ground was more than moonlit sand and he could make out the city coming up. The maps were pretty good, and they'd had a straight shot in, so he knew where to look for the airstrip. That had been his worst fear, flying southwest, that he would pick the wrong spot to set down and then have to hop somewhere else.

However, there it was.

Finn tapped Hans on the arm and pointed. Together, they leaned the plane over to the right enough to line her up. Lot of work, some mornings.

Damn thing flew like a truck, too.

Finn looked back at the two ladies he was transporting.

"Kharga Oasis, coming up," he said.

Miss Shirazi—Zareen—nodded and checked her wristwatch. Finn already had.

"We're running ahead of schedule," she said. "Will anyone be awake?"

"I'd be happy to wake someone up," Finn grinned.

He had pushed getting here. Burned more fuel than necessary, running closer to one-thirty than the usual one-oh-seven *Cerberus* liked to cruise at. Southern fringe of Cairo to Kharga was marked around three hundred and twenty miles. They'd done the run in two and a half hours.

If he could land and refuel in under an hour, *Cerberus* should be able to lift off again with a full load and only minimal complaints.

Clouds overhead looked promising, if only because they might make the air heavier with water.

Today might be the one day in his flying life he was happy for an out-of-season storm.

Cerberus rode light this morning, in spite of all the weight, like a happy puppy going to the park. All he had to do was aim the nose and let the big beast do the work, pushing the nose down into the long glide path, since they were already more or less lined up with the runway.

Back home, he'd catch hell for not doing a quick flyby first, just to make sure everything was clear, but he was in a hurry. And the runway itself was a long, clear stretch of light-colored stone, dirt, and sand with a few outbuildings showing up like pimples, so he'd know if someone wanted to take off.

After all, what fool wanted to go flying at dawn?

What other fool?

He'd never been to Kharga Oasis before, but there weren't that many options for where you might store fuel, so he aimed to hit the nearest edge of the runway and only taxi as far as those buildings on his right.

Worse come to worst, he could refuel himself and leave a note with a promise to repay them later. Or hide some money.

Something.

Zareen was in a hurry, and Finn didn't like surprises.

He reached over and touched the butt of his pistol, just to reassure himself that it was there. He hadn't bothered to put it back next to the seat.

Didn't see the use, since Zareen had her Mauser on her hip.

If the locals wanted to see him as some bizarre air pirate, that was just tough.

Somebody wanting to cause Finn trouble today was biting off more than he could probably chew.

Hans looked over and rolled his eyes, but the Kraut was like that.

"Seriously?" the big man asked in German.

Finn shrugged.

"Beats the alternative," Finn answered in the same tongue.

"The alternative is flying tourists between Berlin and Hamburg," Hans laughed. "Wearing a pressed suit with a cute little cap on your head."

"Shoot me now," Finn shuddered.

The Italians had been much looser about those sorts of things. As long as the plane had the stupid logo painted on the tail, they didn't even really care all that much if Finn had shaved on any given day. Or wore a cap like a railroader.

Still, time to land. Finn spent a couple of minutes concentrating on the automatic steps, getting everything set just right to come in hot and roll down the long airstrip.

Hopefully, no camels decided to wake up right now and amble across in front of him.

That would end the trip real quick.

And touchdown.

The big struts flexed and the wheels rolled. That was the advantage of how *Cerberus* was built. Big wheels, high propellers, and overall design made it fantastic as a bush plane, able to land on any sort of runway cleanly.

He drilled back on the power and taxied the beast towards what he hoped were flight hangars with a fuel tank, or maybe even a tanker truck. He was guessing he needed about half a tank of gas, so around one hundred and eighty gallons.

They rolled to a stop.

The place looked peaceful.

Almost dead.

The Oasis in the distance was pretty, but it didn't look

like anybody was stirring, and he was too far away to hear the morning call to prayer.

Finn cut the engines and silence fell.

Nothing.

He rose and made his way aft, smiling at the two ladies as he went by. He opened the door and climbed out, with both women right behind him.

Hans would open the top hatch and check the tanks. That was how it always went with them as a team. Finn talking to the locals. Hans talking to the bird.

It worked.

Except that there was nobody around.

The closest building had a big bay door on it, presumably to keep sandstorms back a little. There was a regular door next to it, which he tried.

Locked.

Crap.

Zareen surprised him by walking over to the big door and lifting it up.

Unlocked.

Double crap.

Her sarcastic grin didn't help.

Nor did Ghada's.

Finn looked inside and smiled.

Thank God.

An old Fairchild KR-34 biplane. Probably even older than *Cerberus*. Given the location, he'd have guessed it as a mail plane, although it didn't have any markings on it.

Finn stepped into the hangar and looked around.

No fuel truck handy.

This building was attached to the one next to it with an interior door, so Finn went through into the other space.

Empty.

Crap.

He went back to the first and finally found what he was looking for. Just a big tank on the ground marked gasoline on the side, half hidden under a tarp.

He tapped the side and it reverberated nicely, so Finn opened the cap and looked in.

Almost full, which was good, since it looked like it would only hold about two hundred gallons total.

"Now what, Finn?" Zareen asked.

"Now, we find someone," he said, turning to walk back out the bay door into the morning sun.

Hans was up on top of the big, cantilevered wing, all set to start filling tanks.

Finn looked in the direction of the city.

Nobody was stirring over there. Not even lights.

Hell, not even camels.

He wondered if he'd stepped through some weird door. Flown through it, like they did in those Saturday morning serials at the cinema or something, except there hadn't been any storm up there to drop him in some other world.

Just crisp morning air. The nicest kind to fly through.

Finn looked over at Hans and caught the shrug.

Crap.

He turned to Zareen.

"How big of a hurry are we in?" he asked carefully.

She still picked up on something in his voice. Or maybe his face.

"What did you have in mind?" she asked.

Ghada hadn't emerged from the garage, so it was just the two of them for a moment, which felt weird.

"We can start pumping now, and hope someone comes

along," Finn said. "And that they don't arrest us for stealing fuel, which is technically what we're doing until someone comes along and gives us permission. I have no idea how long that might take."

He walked back towards the little biplane and put a hand on the tail. Zareen followed.

"I'm guessing this is a mail plane, since I doubt there are that many Brits around here just flying for fun," Finn continued. "*Cerberus* will probably drain that fuel tank. What do we do if we're done and nobody has shown up yet? If you leave money, I'm sure it vanishes by the time the guy who actually owns the plane shows up to see it. Do we leave a promissory note instead?"

Because yeah, that was just what he wanted to be when he grew up.

An Air Pirate. Or something equally stupid.

Zareen hadn't figured it out before now, either, but she really didn't look like a woman that was all that familiar with the sorts of things you had to do when flying from backwoods locations.

No, she looked like the kind of woman who had chilled champagne delivered to her table at lunch to go with the caviar, instead of beans from a can and warm water.

At least the way she bit her lip was cute.

Made her look sixteen, instead of a grown woman in her early twenties. Still, cute.

Finn decided to just start his career in piracy now, rather than waiting for the Mounties to show up. He walked to the tank and found the pump. There was a long enough hose, so maybe the fellow who owned the thing occasionally filled up folks parked outside.

Worst outcome, Finn figured he could pump a couple of

his barrels empty from inside *Cerberus*, drag them over here and refill them. Be a pain in the ass to get them back onto the plane, but there were four of them.

He'd make it work.

Zareen was still deep in thought, following him around like a puppy, so Finn grabbed the hose and started dragging. Ghada watched, but she didn't look like a mechanic.

Outside, the air was still and had a little chill to it. The sky was gray and overcast, but he didn't know if that was some sort of bizarre marine layer, this far inland at the base of the nearby mountains, or an actual storm front coming through.

Every second was one wasted, so he walked over to where Hans reached a hand down and tossed the end of the hose up to the man.

Come to think of it, air pirate would only fall about in the middle, considering some of the stupid and illegal things he'd done since the end of the war.

Thank God for statutes of limitations. And national borders.

Finn went back to the tank and unlocked the pump itself. It was a strange, hand-cranked kind, like a mad scientist in a bad movie might make. Still, it was the best he could do.

"Hans, you ready?"

"Go ahead, Finn," the man called back.

Finn started cranking.

Ten gallons per minute, from the size of the thing. This was going to take a while, and he'd be sore.

He continued cranking.

After a few minutes, Ghada stepped into the shade and approached.

"I can take a turn," she said quietly.

Finn thought about it and decided he was fine with that level of suffragism. He would need to be able to use his arms to get a fully loaded *Cerberus* off the ground. If all four of them took turns, it might only take twenty or thirty minutes to do this.

He nodded and stepped back. She took his spot and started the crank turning.

Finn walked outside and glanced at the sun. The clouds were high, so he doubted rain, but he only needed it to stay heavy and cool long enough to get into the air again.

Zareen seemed to be intently watching the town, but nothing moved over there. Finn didn't feel like walking over and knocking on someone's door to ask for permission to do anything. If they cared, they'd come over.

And hopefully not as a posse.

He still hated posses.

Hans emerged from *Cerberus* now. Quiet at the best of times, the big Kraut walked into the garage, presumably to talk to Ghada, leaving Finn with the woman in charge.

"I will write a letter," she said out of the blue.

It took him a couple of seconds to figure out what the hell the woman was rambling about.

About that time, she turned and walked over to *Cerberus*.

"Finn, could you help?" she asked.

He followed. Until they had full tanks, he was just a bystander here, needed to occasionally run the pump.

Zareen had boarded, so he did as well. Her trunks were near the back of the cabin, with the heavy barrels as far forward as he and Hans had been able to get them.

"Could you lift this one please?" she asked, pointing to the smaller trunk on top of the stack.

He figured that was her clothing and stuff, with the

bigger steamer trunk holding whatever the woman needed for her dig.

Whatever she was going to dig for.

He got up next to her, close enough to smell the French perfume she was wearing, and got both hands around the thing. More awkward than heavy, he lifted, bumping into Zareen slightly as he did, almost pressing her into the bulkhead accidentally.

"Sorry about that," Finn said.

There wasn't any space close, so he waddled over to the nearest barrel and set it down there for now.

Zareen had opened the bottom trunk. Modern steamer, designed to be set on its side and filled with drawers and maps and stuff a pretty archaeologist needed to find dead people in the Egyptian sand.

She pulled a big envelope out and extracted a piece of paper and an envelope. Finn was close enough to note the Hotel International letterhead, so she'd picked it up when she got to Cairo. At least whoever read it would have a good idea where to find her when they discovered that someone had stolen all their fuel.

She closed up the trunk and located a pen from inside her vest, jotting a quick note in a flowing hand onto the paper before leaving it to dry.

He wasn't close enough to read the words, but she had a pretty hand when she wrote.

She turned and saw him staring. Her blush was cute, too.

Quickly, she picked it up, folded it, and slipped the letter into the envelope.

Finn took that as his cue and picked up her smaller trunk, carrying it carefully back to put it onto the stack and tie it down again. There wasn't much space in here, but she stayed still as he worked, rather than sliding away from him and exiting the plane.

He wasn't sure what to make of that, but she was much too young for him, so he just kept a serious face and nodded to her when he was ready to go.

She exited the plane first, and he followed, trying not to stare too obviously at her bottom. He'd been right, though. Those tight jodhpurs made it look nice as she went into the garage to leave her letter where someone might find it.

Out in the sun again, he looked over at the oasis.

Not even a camel stirring.

Must not be chickens needing to be fed and cattle to milk around here.

Zareen had come back out and was standing midway now, arms wrapped tightly around herself like she was cold.

"You okay?" he asked, stepping close enough to talk, but not to threaten her space.

"I've never brazenly committed such a crime before, Finn." She looked up at him with something like honest fear in her eyes.

He couldn't ever remember being that innocent. Had to have been, at least at some point, but it had been a while.

Finn shrugged.

"Technically, we're not stealing the fuel," he said. "You left an IOU note for the guy that owns the Fairchild, so he can come find you in Cairo when you get back and you can pay him. Stealing's when we just take it because nobody came along to stop us. Totally different situation."

"Do you have much experience, rationalizing those sorts of things?" she asked.

Any other woman, and it probably would have come out

with a sarcastic sneer. With Zareen, it actually sounded like an honest question.

Curiosity, without obvious judgment.

"I fought in the Great War, when I was not much younger than you are now," Finn answered. "Saw a lot of men broken as a result. Not all those wounds are physical. Not all of them heal. Afterwards, a lot of damaged men were standing around, trying to figure out what to do next. US went into a tailspin at first, and then went the other direction, completely over-the-top silly for a decade. Once the bills for that came due, a lot of people were suddenly struggling hard, just to put food on the table."

He paused to study her face, but it was receptive, rather than harsh.

Finn still didn't figure Zareen Shirazi had ever even had to contemplate going to bed hungry.

"Sometimes, you gotta do what you gotta do," he said, repeating the most apt metaphor for the modern age he'd ever heard. "I ain't one of those flaming Marxist types, but anytime a society doesn't take care of the weak and weary, they're setting themselves up for a serious amount of trouble down the line. Ask old King Louie Sixteen about that. Or that Russian Tsar fellow. No, we Americans believe that if you have to do something like this, we should ask why it came to that. And make allowances. You'll pay the fellow back when we find him, but we had a need right now that couldn't wait. Might not be as bad as a hungry baby, but sometimes you have to make allowances. You Brits forget that, or maybe don't like human empathy all that much."

"How dare—" she started to yell, but Finn cut her off.

"I've known a lot of Australians over the years," he snapped. "Them folks didn't all choose to sail to the far end of the world to start a new life. Government sentenced them there for a crime. Americans think you can make amends, do the right thing, and be forgiven for it afterwards."

He watched the heat flare in her eyes. Hard and angry, but she'd never broken the law before. Probably never broken any law, looking at her. That kind of money served to insulate a person. Make them immune to having to understand what poor kids from the wrong side of the tracks might have to do to get by.

However, something got through. Her eyes softened.

Finn's still felt like angry diamonds, but she'd asked.

And he didn't suppose he'd said that much on the topic in a long time. Maybe ever.

Must like her or something.

She wasn't a bad egg, just a little princess having to make her way out in the big, bad world for the first time.

"Forgiveness, huh, Finn?" she asked, in a voice with only a little of the tartness and anger behind it.

"Okay, so maybe I'm a little of a Red, but not so much that I want to tear it all down, like some of them folk." He tried to shrug it off. "But there's something to be said for the saying *From each according to his ability, to each according to his need.* That sort of thinking and this wasn't a crime. This was a need. And you'll make it right later. Correct?"

"Yes," she said. "Yes I will, but you're also right in the implication that I've never really faced the world before this. Never had to make those decisions."

"You're doing pretty good now," Finn replied with another shrug. "You've got us this far. In a while, if nobody comes along, we'll keep going and find whatever it is you were looking for. Or at least where it's been. Then Hans and

I will haul you back to Cairo, or at least someplace civilized enough that you can go on with your life."

He walked away at that point. He figured he'd said enough, anyway. Woman might have chosen to get mad at that. Might still. Didn't make it one bit less true.

Finn wandered in to relieve Ghada, but Hans already had, so he turned and walked back towards *Cerberus*, nodding silently at Zareen as he went by.

She was deep in thought, and he didn't figure she needed more earthquakes in her life this morning.

He'd go check on the tanks. They'd be getting close to filling the first one soon.

And then it would be time to find the desert sky again.

CHAPTER THIRTEEN

Zareen still wasn't sure if she should be angry at Finn or thank him for walking her into this situation and then through to the other side. Certainly neither of her two families would ever rationalize brazen theft the way he did.

But at the same time, neither of them understood poverty.

Or transportation to Australia.

She supposed that an American from a frontier place like Montana might have a radically different approach to such things. More emotionally flexible.

Not living the insulated life of a literal princess might have something to say about that.

After a time, nobody had come. She had even taken a turn at the pump, but it was quickly obvious that she didn't have the strength or the endurance of the others to make a meaningful contribution, so she had simply stood to one side to offer encouragement and keep watch for a man who never came.

The tanks on the plane were full before the pump ran dry.

At that point, she had watched Finn and Hans put everything meticulously away, with her letter resting carefully atop the tank, weighed down by a metal aircraft part she couldn't identify, so it wouldn't blow away or get lost.

Nothing.

Nobody.

She couldn't imagine that the entire Oasis was still asleep, but nobody had deigned to come out here to see what might be happening, so eventually the four of them found themselves aboard the plane, with the engines roaring their excitement to take to the air again.

Finn had even taxied the craft towards the far end of the airstrip, closest to the little town, and elicited no response, so he turned it back into the sun and let those three, magnificent horses run.

As before, she had been convinced that *Cerberus* could never make the end of the strip and lift, but the plane did. Leapt into the sky, alone in the morning sun.

She had lost a day in planning, not understanding that the weight of the craft had been so close to the margin of error. However, they had now picked that day up again, and she would hopefully be to Gabal El Uweinat around lunch time.

Zareen looked forward to overflying the area and seeing if there was anything that spoke of an alien spaceship landing out here. Or, if the rumors were true, it having been destroyed in one of the valleys, possibly as a result of some unknown battle.

How many alien worlds were there? Was Earth a little-visited place, or were there many aliens secretly walking among them, even today?

Nobody had anything more than hints and suggestions.

The Man With No Face was known to express an unexpected interest in all things Gilf Kebir, but also Gabal El Uweinat. And Hassanein's other notes had suggested things that belied simple explanation.

She'd never felt safe enough to consider traveling to Siberia to investigate Tunguska, but there were other places where people had reported what were best described as unknown flying ships.

And in an era where the fastest aircraft were limited to only a few hundred miles per hour, something that could fly faster than sound itself suggested alien technology.

Or at least something so incredibly advanced that she had to know more. His Majesty's Government demanded that.

"Okay, Zareen," Finn called from just in front of her. "We've made sky. What is our course?"

Zareen took a deep breath and steadied herself. So much was riding on what came next.

"Two hundred and thirty degrees, headed west-south-west," she said in a voice that felt like it wanted to strangle in her throat. "Your destination is Gabal El Uweinat, located at 21°52′29″N by 24°54′16″E. It's technically located in Libya, just west of the Sudan border, a little south of where the Egypt-Sudan-Libya border connects on a map."

"What are we expecting to find there?" Finn asked her, leaning inward and turning his head back enough to look directly at her.

"I'm not sure," she said, honestly.

She wasn't sure. Theories, rumors, and hints didn't add up to surety.

"Well, I can't land on the side of a mountain," Finn said, his face looking a little cross.

"Oh," she blinked, forgetting how little she had told the man up until now. "There is a mountain, on the southeast, but there is a ring of them, when drawn on maps. Reports show two wadis entering from the Libyan side, at three hundred and three hundred fifty degrees, more or less. According to reports I have seen, the north wadi empties out into a valley half a mile wide and several miles long."

"That's where you want to dig?" Finn asked.

"That's where I would like you to fly over, so we can see if there are any interesting places that we need to investigate. Very few Westerners have been here. Only Hassanein, Bagnold, and Marchesi have led expeditions that have made it this far."

"What's there?" he asked.

"Jabal Arkanu to the northwest, and Gabal El Uweinat just southeast of that," she said. "The rest is open desert, save for a few mountainous plateaus we will cross over as we go."

"No, lady," Finn said, his voice growing a little harder. "Why all the effort to get there? And the people chasing you? Somebody bury gold or something out there? Pirate treasure maps and things like that?"

Zareen caught her breath, and her tart response. Finn was probably more right than he knew, but she wasn't sure what to tell him.

"Nothing so lucky, Finn," she temporized. "I want to look around and see if the things Hassanein reported make it worth coming back for a formal dig later. The kind that included either camel caravans, or perhaps aircraft resupply."

"Middle of nowhere, if you ask me," Finn grumbled. "Damned nice place to quietly set up a military base, though, if you were wanting to hit Italian targets, or maybe keep them from doing an end run of all the British Army farther north. Assuming a war's coming, which everyone does."

Zareen shrugged with her palms up and tried her best to look innocent.

Certain elements of the British government that had secretly supplied her with funds along the way were investigating that exact scenario, with the expectation of an Axis attack at some point. You had the French south in Chad and Niger, in fact, occupying the entire Sahara belt west of Sudan. Gabal El Uweinat was exceptionally well-situated to intercept something like that. Or initiate it.

However, Hassanein had reported other things. They hadn't made it into his book, but others on the expedition had reported sights that they didn't understand. Something partly covered by sand that had looked like a vehicle of some sort. Then wind had covered it up again overnight, and the expedition didn't stay in place long enough to go digging.

Other rumors had connected with the place, including the Man With No Face in Cairo, though she had never had a chance to talk to him and find any sort of truth.

Zareen wanted to investigate what sounded like a crashed spaceship wreckage before she confronted the being who might have arrived aboard it. Beauchêne would have other motives, but the man was a fascist, intend on conquering the world so that people would recognize his long-overlooked genius.

She doubted he would last long. Mussolini and Hitler both had charisma. The Japanese had an entire warrior culture set on their course. Beauchêne, like the rest of his countrymen, were hopelessly behind the times, culturally, socially, and technologically.

Not that she would share many of her secrets with the British, either.

Zareen Shirazi, like so many of her cousins, longed for the day when Persia would rise up again and be a truly powerful, modern nation. A century of misrule by the Qajar, plus all the meddling by the British, Ottomans, and Russians had broken ancient Persia of its power and stripped away most of its northern possessions.

At least a decade of Reza Khan as Shah had begun the slow process of healing.

Still, Zareen would let the British and others pay her to continue his work.

"You're not going to admit or deny it, are you?" Finn asked after a few moments.

"It's probably safer for you and Hans, Finn," she said. "Some parts of the story you simply would not believe, while others are likely to cause you trouble with the authorities later."

"Uh huh," he grunted, disbelieving.

She really didn't know this American man. Or his German mechanic and friend.

She did know that a war was coming. Another Great War, but this one was likely to truly engulf the entire world, drawing in all sides, and threatening her beloved Persia with invasion from every axis.

She needed the secrets of the Man With No Face if she was going to change that.

CHAPTER FOURTEEN

"What do you mean, vanished?" Didier let his voice rise, both in pitch and volume.

The neighbors had finally traveled on, and as far as he knew, either nobody was in the room next to him now, or they were so quiet as to be invisible. At least he could sleep through the night, rather than listen to the twosome over there fornicate so loudly.

Bertrand shrugged, palms up.

"There are several men who fit the description we had for the Man With No Face," Bertrand replied. "My sources have identified more than half a dozen so far, but many of them are locals or people we could disregard once we looked closer. That left the one to investigate deeper."

"But?" Didier demanded.

"Someone warned him, just as we were getting close," the assassin said. "The information I was able to obtain was that someone went to visit the Man With No Face yesterday in the early afternoon. Immediately after that the visitor left, so did our target. Simply got up and walked out of the café without a word. He did not return this morning. Nobody has seen him since then."

"Did she reach him?" Didier asked.

There was only one *she* in this situation. Zareen Shirazi, that never-to-be-sufficiently-damned British woman. He was certain she was a spy. Only the English would use such an eccentric cover, letting the woman wander about as an amateur archaeologist and explorer.

Bertrand shrugged again, uselessly, but Didier understood.

Time and again, she had seemingly wandered into their plans, as if at random, thwarting them or just derailing things with the appearance of purest accident.

Didier wasn't fooled. Not anymore.

Shirazi had come to Cairo seeking information about the Man With No Face, but then had almost immediately gone into the southwest desert from Cairo from other witnesses Didier had interviewed.

What was out there? More importantly, what had she learned?

"I don't know if she reached him," Bertrand said. "I have offered small rewards, but nothing has come up yet. Do we lay a trap and wait for him to return?"

"And her as well," Didier said. "We know the plane that she hired has a predictable range, and the fact that they added enough fuel in barrels to return suggests that there is a specific ring into which she is searching."

"A ring?" Bertrand asked, confusion carved into his thin features.

"They have to be traveling farther than they could reach on half a tank of fuel, else they could have flown back afterwards without needing to refuel. Southwest suggests that they stopped at Kharga. From Kharga, their range is no more than two hundred and fifty miles," Didier explained. Bertrand was canny, but uneducated. A killer, not a scholar. "At the same time, there is nothing out there where they could expect to land that they could expect to find fuel sufficient to continue."

Didier rose now, moving to his traveling valise and opening it. Thumbing through the satchel, he pulled out a map of northern Africa and a compass.

The spy returned to the table and laid the map out. He set the compass and began measuring.

"I assume something further southwest," Didier explained as Bertrand moved closer. "If it was south, they would have flown someplace like Aswan first, then moved on. West, they would have gone to places like Tobruk first."

"What is out there?" Bertrand asked.

On the map, there were vague trails marked, showing ancient caravan routes through the interior, as well as the newer ones that Hassanein had been able to open up through the southern parts of Cyrenaica.

Two hundred and fifty to three hundred miles was a wide band, but nothing stood out. Gilf Kebir was simply too big of a region, but it was mostly just desert out there, with only a few mountain tops that stuck up out of the surrounding sands like American tors in places like Arizona.

"Nothing, as far as I can tell," Didier replied after a time, studying the map, as if it would give up its secrets. "But that is a lie. Somehow, the Man With No Face is connected to a point out here. We must find it and find him. She's gone into the desert, but she should return here, as the manager at the hotel told me that everything of hers has gone into storage. If she cables for them to send it on somewhere, we will know.

Instead, we must redouble our efforts to find the Man With No Face and discover his secret."

"That is a needle in an enormous haystack," Bertrand pointed out.

"That is your job, Bertrand," Didier said.

"And you?"

"I will be setting a trap for Shirazi," he said with a smile.

CHAPTER FIFTEEN

Sun.

Hot and nasty.

Straight up overhead now, as Finn maneuvered around.

From eight thousand feet, the terrain below looked almost like a bullseye. Concentric-looking rings of uplifted stone, with the more-southern valley running generally northwest, and the other one to his right.

Finn preferred this valley, as looking at it he could see trees down there. Water would run occasionally on the surface and maybe there was a stream under the sand. He seemed to remember that Zareen had mentioned a spring somewhere nearby, outside the valley itself, but she wanted to be up here, and they didn't even have a bicycle to get around, so he wasn't about to go walking far.

Besides, they had a whole barrel of water that was fresh enough, drawn from the well at the airstrip.

He pointed to a spot on their left and banked a little so Hans could see. Looked flat enough. *Cerberus* was designed for rough landings like this, as long as they didn't run into anything that had been buried shallowly under the sand.

Most of the area below looked like rock that had been largely ground down anyway, with sand blown in and washed down the valley by what little water accumulated.

"You've seen them both, Zareen," Finn called over the dull rumble of the engines. "Which one did you want us to land at?"

They had plenty of fuel left in the tanks, so he wasn't too worried about having to refuel if he had to land now and then hop back up later. He just didn't want to walk.

"The northern one," Zareen answered, because of course she did.

At least she'd made up her mind before landing and looking around.

Finn nodded to Hans and suffered the man's grin.

"Told you," Hans said just loud enough that Finn was the only person who would hear it.

Ghada might be able to read lips, but not hear.

He should know better than to make bets with the big Kraut, even after all this time they'd been partners in crime and adventure.

They both leaned into the wheel and nosed the beast back around to the right. There was a valley running around the ring that would let him start his descent, and then give them most of the valley itself to use as a downwind run.

Today, he was being proper, because he wasn't in a hurry and had no idea what he was going to find when he dropped *Cerberus* down on the sand.

Actually, there were three valleys he could pick from with the northern of the two mouths opening and then splitting, but the northernmost one was all wadis and channels. The middle one really opened out into a nice, flat space where he could work. That was the one she really meant.

If there was any water underneath, in a spring or an aquifer you could dig to, this would be the perfect place to set up a hidden base if you were of a mind to.

Finn couldn't see the Brits using a woman as a spy, but at the same time, nobody else would either, so it might be the perfect cover.

Not his job to worry. And if she was working for the Brits, they'd be on the same side anyway if the Italians decided to get stupid.

More stupid.

Italian stupid, like the kind that had left him stranded in Cairo, owed money and in possession of an aircraft that they seemed to have forgotten about.

Of course, if they wanted it back, they were welcome to come down here to wherever the hell he was and chat.

It helped that Hans was an even less charitable kind of guy.

Downwind went well, but Finn was feeling a little extra careful today, so he orbited everything once more, just to be sure. Hans agreed, or he'd have already been bitching.

There was a nice straight shot in that looked relatively flat. Enough that *Cerberus* could handle it, and they'd be effectively running empty on the way out later, since most of his takeoff original weight was going to get pumped up into the overhead tanks.

Yeah, this was as good as it was going to get. Pop over these rocks coming in. Split the gap there, leaning a little more to the left as you went in. Flat enough.

"Everybody stand by," Finn called out, just because. "We'll be lining it up and landing shortly. Stay put until I shut the engines down, in case we run into a problem and I have to gun it to clear something."

Of course, anything he ran across here was likely to break something, but they had tools and equipment to fix most of it. And with three engines, they could always limp home on two, or at least get someplace where they could find repairs.

Not like there was anybody within a hundred miles of them right now if they got into trouble. And he sure as hell didn't want to try to walk to wherever to get help.

Finn brought *Cerberus*'s nose around and swooped. They were just barely above stall speed, so he had a clear view. Everything looked good enough. And he'd be happy to be on the ground now, after such a weird day.

"Landing," he called unnecessarily, as the wheel touched and began to spin.

Softly now, he dialed everything back and let the tail drop. Not going for broke, but there were no judges out there today awarding points for neatness or beauty, and he wanted to be stopped as fast as he could, just to reduce the number of unseen rocks he had to drive over.

Better to walk the runway later and get a feel for what he was facing when he had to take off again in a few days, once the women had done whatever the hell lady adventurers needed to come out to the middle of nowhere to do.

He was going to hang his hammock between the wing and the body, like usual, and pretend to be shipwrecked somewhere in the south Pacific and awaiting a rescue ship.

No pretty maids bringing him rum and pineapple drinks, but nobody had hired him to dig in the hot sun and sand, either.

They got landed and came to rest.

Everything was shut down. Happy.

Halfway completed with all this silliness and folderol.

Hans reached a hand across Finn's nose, pointing at a spot on their left.

"*Was ist das?*"

CHAPTER SIXTEEN

Asher knew that humans were a complicated, messy group of sentient creatures, still socially regressive enough to believe in wars and violence based on such primitive things as tribalism and religion.

Worse, they were used to wielding underhanded methods to get things, frequently with the explicit threat of violence behind their activities.

How much human civilization was explained by the simply threat of retaliation?

Strangers had come to Cairo.

One group of questions centered on a French industrialist named Didier Beauchêne. He was the most intent on locating the Man With No Face, assiduously sending out an assistant the streets knew simply as Bertrand, to ask questions and offer cash rewards or threats for information.

The second group was somehow driven by an Englishwoman with a Persian name. Zareen Vüsala Shirazi.

His own contacts had portrayed the woman as a noblewoman with a complicated past, an unflagging curiosity, and at least as much money as Beauchêne.

While the Frenchman was driving his inquiries into the bad neighborhoods of Cairo, the woman had departed with alacrity and some secrecy.

In one of those strange coincidences that may or may not make the entire thing part of some grand, literary conspiracy, the aircraft Shirazi had hired was the very one that had previously brought a group of Italian spies into Cairo, from which they had not later departed, as near as several investigative sources could determine.

But chaos was a function of intelligence, so Asher could not determine if the intersection had meaning. Nor could anyone else offer clues.

He did not think that the woman would find anything useful at Gabal El Uweinat, but that was not the same thing as there being nothing there to find. He would have to put out questions among his more trustworthy contacts and see what it was she brought back from the desert, if she did.

Hopefully, there was nothing there that would influence the British authorities to get directly involved.

If that happened, Asher had already made plans that would see him walking on a winding path through the hottest, driest parts of the desert itself, southwesterly, until he eventually crossed the Sahara and ended up in one of the French colonies along the Ivory Coast.

Sub-optimal, but better than being found out and having his mission fail in the most spectacular way possible.

Asher was not programmed for self-preservation at all costs, as some robots were, but he enjoyed existence and had learned so much about humans that needed to be communicated to the Durren, even if he ended up being dismantled afterwards.

And it wasn't as if he could build a hyper-relay capable of sending a message home. Human science and metallurgy were still merely physical. And he was a sociologist, not an engineer.

In order to build something himself, he risked accelerating Earth's technological development far in advance of their social structure's strengths.

Further.

He wasn't even sure if the war everyone was expecting soon would engulf the entire world and drag them back down to a pre-industrial state.

If so, he would start a new file and witness the destruction of a relatively primitive industrial society back down to wherever they landed.

That sort of development was actually likely to bring the Durren looking, if all the new radio signals from Earth ceased one day.

Then Asher figured he could catch a ride to prison.

For today, he had to evade the watchers.

Hood and turban and mask had been sufficient to hide him from outsiders when Egyptians preferred to mind their own manners, but the locals had a better network than the Westerners gave them credit for. Cairo was a large town to hide in. Ankara or Istanbul would be places he could flee to, later, but there he would be a complete outsider for a time.

A man approached Asher's most recent hiding place.

Mina was his name. Asher had dealt with him previously.

Usually mutually beneficially, as well.

Mina paused at the entryway to the small alley where

Asher waited. It was late morning now, based on his internal clocks rather than the amount of sun.

Asher emerged and stood near enough to Mina to talk without raised voices.

"What news?" he asked the man.

"*The Assassin* grows nervous," Mina chuckled.

They had taking to calling the Frenchman named Bertrand *The Assassin*, after it became known that he had tried to kill the Englishwoman and been driven off when she nearly shot him.

As near as Asher could tell from the tone, it was more a title of derision than anything.

"How so?" Asher asked simply.

Mina preferred a direct conversation, most of the time.

"Rewards for clues have gone up," Mina replied, quoting some rates that suggested that *The Assassin* and his superior were growing *something*.

Nervous? Desperate? Angry?

Asher had money stashed in a number of locations against need. Not all of them were in banks where he might be required to produce his papers, the ones that had been forged at a previous date.

He slipped Mina an English Pound note now, saw the man's eyes grow big.

"This is too much for such simple news," Mina exclaimed.

"For now, perhaps," Asher replied. "But they will perhaps offer more in the future, and I would prefer to keep them out of my private business. Not many men in Cairo can find me now, and I would prefer to keep it that way."

"Ah, yes, the voice of wisdom, my friend," Mina said.

"And they are strangers as well. Should we perhaps make it more difficult for them?"

"Challenging without violence," Asher replied.

"Is it true that you refuse to do harm to any living creature?" Mina asked.

Asher considered his reply carefully, as he always did when asked this question.

"It is not my first preference, if it can be avoided," Asher said. "Circumstances have rarely been so bad that it became a necessity, but I retain that option."

"Rumor suggests that a brigand attempted to assault you two days ago in an alley," Mina offered carefully. "That he struck you with a club, but you took it away from him and then broke it with your bare hands."

Asher would have smiled, had he the physiology to allow it. Weirdly, this was one of those odd situations where his programming not only allowed him to lie, but actively encouraged it.

Anything, in the process of protecting his identity from discovery.

And it did not even call for a particularly egregious lie.

"You should not believe everything you hear, Mina," Asher said. "I merely scared the man off with my words. If he chooses to tell something other than that, such a thing is between him and Allah The All-Merciful."

Mina smiled at him.

"Such is the man's reputation for honesty that nobody believed him, Asher," he nodded. "But I will let it be known that the Frenchman and his poodle are no friends of ours, even as they seek to spite the English. Do you have rumors you do wish to spread, to distract them?"

Asher had not considered the tool of using lies offensively. It was not in his basic programming, but he could see the intrinsic value in a small lie now that worked to prevent a larger problem later. And with the right timing, it might draw his pursuers away for long enough for him to break more of his embedded programming rules.

What kind of being would he turn into, after enough time spent around humans?

"You might suggest that I took passage on a ship to England or France, if any are available at Alexandria or Cairo. Germany, if you are feeling especially cruel, as the Germans are likely to be less forgiving of troublemakers."

The way Mina's eyes lit up suggested that Asher had indeed found a soft spot into which lies and innuendo might breed and feed.

It was a violation of his programming to cause humans to be subjected to violence, but he was also supposed to protect himself from discovery, and the generic value of human life did not supersede that.

On the scale, misdirection was a small thing.

"It shall be as you suggest, Asher," Mina said, bowing with a chuckle and walking away.

Somewhere, Asher suspected that an entire industry had just been spawned, expressly for the purpose of playing an elaborate practical joke on the Frenchman and his allies.

Hopefully, it would be enough.

CHAPTER SEVENTEEN

She had made it. They were technically trespassing in Libya, or Cyrenaica, depending on who it was you asked, but Zareen had actually gotten here. That place where so many vague rumors and idle chatter suggested that something awaited her.

Even better, Hans Fertig had seen something when they rolled to a stop.

Nobody knew what it was, but light reflected off of something, in a place where nothing of the like should have.

Even more interesting, it wasn't visible from the ground, whatever it was.

They had shut down the engines on *Cerberus* and waited for Finn. Once he opened the door, they had all trooped outside to look, but there was nothing. Zareen had paused to grab a satchel much larger than a lady's purse and more useful, made of stout cotton duck and filled with the sorts of things she wanted close at hand out here, including spare magazines for her Mauser.

Muttering a profanity under his breath, Hans returned to the cockpit, but Zareen had remained below. She motioned Ghada to stay nearby and walked several paces to the left, trying to spot something on the wall of the valley where they had landed.

Behind her, Finn stood in the shade of the wing for a moment, before curiosity apparently got the better of the man and he joined her.

"Left some," Hans suddenly called out, sliding the pilot's window open and pointing.

Zareen obliged after making sure her cap was in place. She had chosen a kepi modeled on the French Foreign Legion today, short-brimmed with a long piece of coarse white cotton cloth hanging all the way around in back to cover her ears and neck from the sun.

"Ja, there," Hans said next. "Walk straight away now."

Zareen turned to study the plane and then rotated in place. She found a spot on the wall in front of her and began to walk carefully, the ground slowly rising as she did.

Finn had landed them nearly at the center of the wide valley, slightly left of center as the axis went. There wasn't much slope here as she walked.

"Farther left," Hans yelled behind her.

Zareen adjusted herself a little and continued.

"Yes, *gut*, there," he called.

Ghada looked fierce. Finn looked put upon. Zareen just hoped that something interesting awaited, as Hans remained in the shade of the aircraft.

It was not cooler there, but he was at least out of the direct sun at this moment.

She reached into her bag and pulled out the metal canteen, formerly British Army issue, that she had picked up in Alexandria, to replace the one lost in the mad departure from Lisbon on the first flight she had been able to book. The water was warm, but clean. She had added a pinch of salt, as well. Not enough to taste, but to keep her going in the desert heat.

"There," Finn said abruptly.

Zareen turned towards the man, to see his eyes locked in on something she was apparently too short to see. His arm went out and he adjusted his line of walking a bit, so she followed in his wake.

She'd been surprised that the man accompanied them this far from the airplane, but perhaps the riddle had overcome his reservations.

Twenty paces on, she saw it as well. Sunlight reflecting off a polished surface.

Except that there should be none here, unless Hassanein had come here and left something. She knew that there had been other explorers as well, but most of them had been focused on the southeast, finding the best path to the top of the Gabal El Uweinat itself.

Men and the need to stand at the top of a meaningless rock, just for the ego of having done it.

Zareen preferred to find the mountain's secrets, rather than to raise a cairn as the others had done.

As she got close, Zareen drifted her path farther to her left, since she could see now where something was half-buried in the sand at the base of where the wall rose.

It was not a cliff face, but a wall nonetheless, canting back at perhaps sixty degrees or more here and too steep to walk up without ropes and harnesses.

Something about the face of the wall also looked wrong.

She stopped and studied it. Ghada did as well.

Finn walked another few steps before stumbling to a stop and turning around.

"What?" he asked.

"There," she replied, almost as brusquely. "Is it my imagination, or did something strike the mountain hard enough to scar the stone?"

Finn turned in place, the object at the base forgotten.

"Impact," Ghada said simply. "Pieces fractured off, while others were weakened. Gravel and shards slid down and landed."

"What the hell might have done that?" Finn asked.

Zareen smiled and began to walk again. The American pilot would not believe her, even if she tried to explain it, so it wasn't worth trying.

After all, he considered himself just an employee, hauling her and Ghada for a fee and returning them to safety later. There was no reason to draw him in deeper.

The conspiracy was already strange and complicated enough.

The pile below made sense now. It was rubble from above that had fallen, along with sand that had blown in, swirled, and was occasionally pushed away as well.

The light reflecting would only be visible on a fairly narrow line and elevation, and only for a certain stretch of time each day, when the sun was overhead enough to align with a gap.

Zareen knelt as she got close, studying the gap of perhaps a foot between two jagged hunks of stone larger than she was.

This was exactly where she would expect desert snakes and such to take refuge from the heat. Or perhaps smaller creatures hiding from snakes.

She reached into her bag and pulled out a wooden club

she carried specifically for such a thing, an inch around and eighteen inches long.

She stuck it into the gap quickly and held it, waiting to see if anything struck at it.

After a few moments, she moved it around.

Nothing.

Zareen looked closer.

The sun had already drifted enough that the little gap was now in shadow. She wondered if they would have missed it entirely, had they landed any earlier or later in the day.

The object appeared to be glass. However, when she tapped on it, it had a thunk more like metal, except that she could see more sand through it.

Zareen used the stick like a tool now, probing the edge where the rocks vanished under the accumulated sand, pulling it towards her until she saw an edge. Slipping the tip of the rod under that edge, she was able to lever it up.

The whole thing gave way at once when she did, sand cascading away.

Nothing jumped out and bit her, which was closer to what Zareen had been expecting.

She took a deep breath and reached out with her left hand, ready to smash something if necessary.

The glass was light.

Zareen slipped the rod back into her bag and considered the thing she held.

It had a slight curve to it when she pulled it out of the gap and stepped back to stand up. Emerald cut in shape, half again as long as it was wide, and even curved like such a stone, when she considered it. Perhaps eight inches wide by a foot or so long, with a rise of about two inches were she to lay it flat.

Transparent, but not glass. It didn't feel right under her fingers. She tapped it and it was more like the side of a battleship than a champagne bottle.

She could see holes all the way around the rim of the glass, now that she was paying attention. Like the sort of thing where you would press rivets. And one end was still riveted to a section of something that was metal.

Maybe metal.

Gray, at least. Again, much lighter than steel or even aircraft aluminium. Held in place with two rivets, but the remaining metal was torn, as one might tear a simple piece of paper.

"Looks like something off *Cerberus*," Finn volunteered, standing next to her opposite Ghada but specifically not touching the thing in her hands.

"How so, Finn?" Zareen asked.

"Permanently set in place with these pins," Finn replied. "But you need to see out. Think of the windows in the sides of the plane that let you see the terrain as we're flying over."

Zareen grasped the metal piece in her hand and attempted to bend it, but it was as solid as granite in her hands.

She stepped back and considered the place on the wall, perhaps fifteen feet above her head, where the face was scarred by damage.

Had this thing been driven into the granite hard enough to spall off chunks? It was so light. Or was there a larger piece of something beneath the stone at her feet?

It had been suggested that the Man With No Face was a traveler from distant lands. Other rumors had centered on this particular mountain.

How far away had the man come from?

Zareen considered the rough piles of granite where this object had lain hidden. She tapped the glass against the largest one.

It did not surprise her when the glass refused to crack, even as light as it was.

She'd held champagne flutes that felt more durable. But none of them gave the impression of such solidity.

She tapped harder. Small pieces of granite fractured off the stone, but the glass remained unmarked.

"So what is it?" Finn asked, genuinely curious now, rather than sarcastically superior.

"As you said, it appears to be part of an aircraft, Finn," Zareen replied.

"Did it crash here?" he asked, stepping back and looking at the immediate terrain and that mark on the wall in a new light. "Slam into the face and crumple?"

"That is what we're looking into, Finn," Zareen smiled up at the man. "For now, I'd like us to set up something of a camp nearby, so Ghada and I can investigate, starting here. You and Hans can prepare *Cerberus* for our return journey and then take care of whatever maintenance tasks are necessary. In a few days, I'll know enough to determine whether we should indeed return with a larger expedition."

"Why all the secrecy, lady?" he asked, his face scrunching down now as he apparently began to think deeper thoughts than the man was accustomed to on a normal day. "It is something special? The Germans lose an experimental aircraft over the Egyptian desert or something?"

"Something," she agreed ambivalently.

She didn't dare tell the man her own theories, let alone those of the men and women who provided the funding.

After all, the smaller the number of people who were involved, the better.

Zareen was sure Finn Severijns was not a spy, nor Hans Fertig, but she didn't know how they might react to the suggestion of little green men from Mars, or something equally mysterious, walking around on Earth.

CHAPTER EIGHTEEN

Finn wanted to grumble, but it was his own damned fault.

Intrigued by the thing Zareen had found, he'd found a strip of cloth to wrap around his head and neck like a weird turban and helped her and Ghada dig in the sand all afternoon.

Even Hans had gotten into it eventually, but those three big hunks of granite weren't moving until someone brought in some heavy equipment to do the job.

They hadn't found anything else down there, but they could only go so far into the sand at this point.

Damn that bug of curiosity that had bit him.

But it had been hot.

Broiling.

Desert sun with almost no breezes.

It would have been nice to have had those clouds from Kharga follow him, but they'd burned off and drifted north almost as soon as *Cerberus* had lifted off, so he wasn't sure if the gods wanted to make sure he got here, or just wanted to see him sweat.

Eventually, they had stopped and the women had put up a nice tent. Hadn't even needed his help to do it. It would have been pleasant to have a nice little fire, but there was no wood around here they could burn.

Well, not unless he felt like walking several miles gathering it.

Afternoon was wearing on.

Ghada had brought a Coleman lantern from the States, so they had light after the sun went down. Better than the moon and stars against the white sand, anyway.

Temperatures were going to drop soon, but he wondered what all this plug of granite was going to be like. Would that much stone hold extra heat and keep this basin warm all night?

Hans was asleep inside *Cerberus*. The women had retired to their tent.

Finn had slung his hammock and found a blanket to ward off the coming chill. These day, he couldn't really sleep on the ground, and even beds were iffy, depending on how soft the mattress was.

Too much time spent in this hammock, hanging from the side of the plane anytime there wasn't rain, or because some idiot in Rome forgot to make arrangements for hotel rooms for him and Hans, or hadn't paid someone.

Or something.

He really hadn't been all that surprised when Aurora Italia Airlines ceased operations.

Hell, if anything, he was kinda surprised they'd survived as long as they had. Of course, some of the travelers he'd been transporting from Rome to other places didn't look much like tourists, so he'd always wondered if the Italian government was involved or something.

Especially that last batch that he'd dropped off in Cairo when the ground office got fired by telegram.

But it was evening, and he was tired. Finn just let the light breeze rock him.

Zareen and Ghada's tent wasn't all that far away. It had been too heavy to haul the hundred or so yards up to where she wanted to dig, even if Finn had felt like volunteering.

Plus, if something happened, he wanted them closer.

You never know what kind of strange animals might be running around inside this basin, especially if there was enough water to support an ecosystem, however thin it might be.

Hopefully, nothing bigger than mice and the kinds of birds or snakes that might hunt them. There hadn't been eagles or such in the skies when he'd been approaching, but Finn had also been paying attention to the hills and terrain below him, rather than things in the air.

Trees and such in the other valley suggested that things would live there, but the hike would be a few miles if he felt like an adventure, which was not that high on his list.

For now, Ghada had already retired. Zareen was studying that weird piece of glass she'd extracted.

Wasn't Bakelite, or anything like that, so he had no idea what it might be. She'd let him hold it, but it had seemed impossibly light.

Make an aircraft out of that sort of thing and you'd be able to fly pretty fast, just because the engines didn't have nearly as much weight to lift.

And as tough as it was, one of those new all-metal interceptor fighter craft would be able to pull all sorts of crazy maneuvers. Far better than *Cerberus* could, to say nothing of the canvas, wood, and wire art installations he'd flown during the war, where a stiff wind or a too-tight turn might end up cracking something.

He studied the woman now, seated in her campaign chair under the light provided by the lantern, itself hanging from a tent pole.

Young. Amazingly fresh and unworldly in some ways. Enough so that he felt like an old man at forty, just enjoying her wit and beauty.

Extremely smart. Way too educated for an English noblewoman. Especially one of those, since those folk didn't usually believe in letting women study too much, convinced it would somehow sully their femininity.

Additionally, she was also half-Arab of some sort, although he'd never asked. It was obvious from the bones in her face, the color of her skin, and the shape of her eyes.

None of his damned business, though. That much she'd made clear, the few times she'd looked up and caught him staring. No blushing damsel there.

No, hardness came into her eyes, like he was a threat.

Finn liked dumber women, frankly. Curvier, too, when he had a chance. Less likely to challenge you to intellectual combat or correct your manners and ignorance, either way.

As his dad had told him many times: *Never chase a woman smarter than you. At some point, you'll have to roll over and talk to her.*

Zareen Shirazi didn't look like the kind of woman who would be happy with a lost bush pilot like him.

Just as well.

He could still study her hands as she studied the artifact, lost inside herself and learning God only knows what. He was just the pilot, like Hans was just the mechanic.

Or something like that.

He shrugged and settled himself back into the hammock.

After a few more minutes, she picked up the lantern and carried it back to her tent.

"Goodnight, Finn," she said as she turned away.

"Goodnight, Zareen," he called back.

She disappeared inside her tent and the lamp went off, plunging everything into darkness.

At least as much darkness as you got when there were no lights to obscure all those stars overhead, or the partial moon trying to replace the vanished sun. His eyes adjusted quickly.

Finn took a deep breath and listened to Hans snoring quietly away inside *Cerberus*. There was just enough of an evening breeze to call itself that without blushing, but not enough to represent much of a threat to anything.

It had been a crazy couple of days. On the other hand, with what they were making from hauling the women around, maybe he and Hans would have enough to get themselves where they could pick up a real gig.

Maybe he'd just start flying mail and cargo in and out of Cairo. Wasn't like there was a lot of competition, and it would keep him employed, at a time when things looked to be getting a little weird up in Europe. And might spill over here.

Of course, how much weirder would it get with Zareen and whatever peculiar aircraft she was digging up? Especially if it was something German and experimental, lost out here.

Probably a good time to make friends with the British Establishment.

Wasn't like the Italians were likely to hire him back at this rate.

No, time to settle things down a little and just make some money.

He needed some quiet in his life.

Thank God there was nobody out here.

CHAPTER NINETEEN

He didn't think he'd been asleep, but a sound caused him to start.

Finn opened his eyes just enough to see sky and an airplane wing, before something flipped him ass over teakettle, dropping him face down into the sand.

He didn't think they had bears in Egypt, but something landed on his back and he couldn't get up.

Finn struggled, and whatever it was shifted wrong. He was able to roll hard and threw the pair of them forward and away, freeing up his legs.

Finn shook his head and decided now would be a good time to get the .45 out, since he was dealing with something.

One hand went up, and then he froze as someone poked him with the long end of a bayonet. Attached to an even-longer rifle.

Several more bayonets.

Several more men.

Desert Bedouins, from their dress, with long robes over the body and their faces covered.

A woman screamed and Finn started to move, but one of the bayonets jabbed him. Just enough to draw a little blood, rather than kill.

"Enough," a voice yelled so loud that Finn heard the echo off the cliff face a moment later.

Silence fell.

Finn dared look over at *Cerberus*, where Hans was emerging with his hands over his head and two more men pointing guns at him.

The other direction, someone had opened the flap of the tent and was shining a light in, with several more men standing here, guns in hand.

"Do not move," the man standing over Finn said in Italian.

Finn didn't really like the Italians all that much right now. Spoke their tongue enough to get by, ordering food, beer, and a room, and that was pretty much it.

Plus, right now, he was seeping blood. Probably ruin the shirt.

"Who the hell are you?" he snapped back at them in English.

"You are English?" the man with the loud voice asked, apparently surprised.

"American," Finn growled up at the man. "The ladies are English."

"Ladies?" he asked, turning on his heel and stomping quickly over to the tent.

A few yells emerged from the tent a moment later. Sounded like Arabic but it was too muffled to make out, followed by the sound of someone getting a solid right cross to the jaw.

There was a particular sound to a good right cross. Nothing else in the world sounded like it.

"What is the meaning of this?" Zareen demanded in that almost-shrill, viciously angry voice that only English women ever seemed to have mastered. "Take your hand off me, you savage."

Finn flinched again, but the man with the rifle pointed at him looked like he might shoot if Finn even breathed heavy right now.

"Who are you people?" Zareen demanded a moment later.

Finn finally saw her emerge from the tent without moving his head.

The man in charge emerged on her heels.

"Awali, drag Abdul out here and disarm him," the man snapped in Arabic, apparently seething with a rage so hot Finn was kind of amazed he wasn't glowing right now.

"You, American, stand up," the man ordered, pushing the guy with the Enfield rifle and bayonet back.

Finn moved slowly, glancing down to realize that his Colt was already gone. That must have been what woke him up, when somebody picked his pocket for the gun. He rose carefully, noting that there were more than a dozen Bedouins around here, all of them with rifles either in their hands or slung on their backs because they had submachine guns or pistols in hand.

Zareen had been sleeping in a cotton shift that was probably thinner than she would have chosen for herself had she been expecting company. You wouldn't have known it from the snarl on her face, though.

Ghada wore something similar. Older and more worn, perhaps, because while Zareen's was barely enough for modesty, Ghada's left very little to the imagination. He hadn't seen the woman without the billowing robes she normally wore, so he hadn't had a chance to appreciate how nicely built Ghada was.

Finn was used to Egyptian women who were either waifs trying to earn a few pounds on the side, or middle-aged *hausfraus* who might weigh as much as he did.

Zareen was on the slender side, tall and lean and elegant.

Ghada reminded Finn of a drill instructor he'd met when he first enlisted, a bulldog, spark plug of a man who looked like one of those cartoons where a tall, skinny man got squished down. Compact, wide, and muscular.

Ghada had that going in spades, with the addition of hips and a nice chest.

Finn decided he couldn't hide behind the two women, as nice as the view was, so he stepped between them and more or less planted himself as close to the tall Bedouin leader as he could without getting punched, shot, or stabbed, depending on who flinched first.

"Is there anyone else?" the man asked in English, rather than Arabic.

"Just the four of us," Finn said, apparently also speaking for the group now as well.

But that might not be all bad. Arab tribesmen tended to have a low opinion of women, keeping them veiled and penned up in the cities. He didn't know what the desert tribes were like, never having been this far from a civilized bar before.

Bizarrely, the man put two fingers to his mouth and whistled, a shrill bird call that echoed across the valley.

"We will take you back to our camp while we figure out what to do with you," he said.

That didn't sound like fun, by any stretch of the imagination, but Finn got to watch the one apparently called Alawi dragging another man out of Zareen and Ghada's tent, the second fool out cold.

Either the man had a glass jaw, or the leader of the tribe had learned how to box at some point.

Finn had boxed a little when he was young. It was the sort of thing you did at that age, but he didn't think he'd last more than a few rounds against the wiry leader. Especially not if he'd taken this Abdul fellow down with one punch.

A sound cut the night. Internal combustion engine.

Seriously? Here?

How?

Or better, why?

Lights came on and a flatbed truck bounced and rumbled down the valley towards them. Finn hadn't seen any encampment in any of the valleys, but he'd been focused on sand. Maybe they'd had a cave or something, except that they had a truck.

Coming this way suggested that maybe they had navigated through the top of the complex, where the various valleys looked like they all connected.

Finn didn't think he'd ever heard of Bedouins in Ford trucks, though.

It braked to a halt with a squeal that caused both Finn and Hans to flinch. Brakes were set wrong. And the engine was running too lean for the elevation, so it tended to misfire a little.

Nothing you couldn't fix with a little maintenance, but Finn supposed that tribesmen off the desert floor might not have learned how to maintain these sorts of things after the war.

"Get in," the leader commanded.

Finn found it educational that the man had a pistol on a belt around his waist, but not in his hands. Like maybe he was waiting for Finn to do something stupid so he could right cross an American pilot, too.

Hans went up into the truck without being prodded. He held a hand down and the two women got lifted up as well.

Finn turned to the leader and steeled himself to get punched. And take it.

"If we're going any great distance, the women will need a blanket or something," he said. "Or you could let them get dressed."

The leader scowled hard enough that Finn clenched his teeth, but the man relented suddenly.

"Grab a blanket from the tent," he ordered one of the men, even as Alawi and someone else lifted an unconscious Abdul over the tailgate and into the bed.

Finn was shocked. Moreso when the man smiled wryly at him.

"We are not savages, American," he said quietly. "Into the truck."

Finn didn't want to be bleeding any more than he was, so he hopped up and took the spot on the side. Zareen and Ghada had their backs to the cab, with him and Hans between the two women and the three Bedouin men who climbed up a moment later. One of the men handed up a quilt that the women used to cover up against the chill and eyes of all the men in the truck.

Horses emerged from the darkness as well, clomping across the night sand quietly, close enough for Finn to see one man leading two strings of desert ponies. He had grown up around Percherons, and other big beasts useful for pulling stumps and dragging logs around, so these horses looked tiny to him, but the leader and most of his band mounted like professional cowboys and the truck began to move, driving farther down the valley towards the northwest.

It was bitterly cold, even as slow as they were moving, so Finn was glad the women had a quilt. Zareen even covered his legs with it as they bounced.

There wasn't much he could do right now that probably didn't end up getting himself shot, so Finn just had to ride his luck at this point.

All he had going for him was the smile on the leader's face, there at the end, and the hopes that the rumors he'd heard about the desert tribes at war with the Italians who had invaded didn't extend to all foreigners.

It was going to be a long night, otherwise.

CHAPTER TWENTY

Zareen had never imagined that there were any of the desert tribes this close to Gabal El Uweinat, even with the newer caravan routes into the Sudan, or she would have found them a more defensible position to camp, as well as made arrangements for there to be someone on watch all night.

As it was, the first sound indicating trouble had apparently been Finn Severijns being dumped out of his hammock by armed tribesmen. There had been three men in the tent when she opened her eyes, knives out and staring at her and Ghada.

One of the men had just worked up the courage to perhaps rape or at least ravage her when their leader had entered and punched him out cold with one blow, so Zareen had her hopes that at least that man was vaguely civilized. Perhaps one of the Senussi leaders that were resisting the Italian occupation of Cyrenaica, with their Emir in exile in Egypt.

Certainly, the coastal cities had been heavily colonized by

Italians, but she had hoped that the war had not come this far south.

At least these men were not friends with the Italian Army, since those people would also start asking questions Zareen would rather not answer.

She watched the leader riding beside the truck, almost exactly behind Finn on a magnificent black horse with an expensive saddle and tack. Her father's side of the family had bred horses, mostly for racing, so she could see the care the man took.

He was a natural horseman, riding easy, even as the truck lumbered and waddled over the sand and rock, eventually emerging from the mountain's basin and down onto the sand, with the peak of Jabal Arkanu just visible on her left as the truck turned south and began to head even deeper into the desert.

How badly had she miscalculated? Was the war indeed this far south? Were the Italians at risk of discovering the secrets of Gabal El Uweinat, even as she herself had just finally found out that there was something to the whispers that had made it as far as Lisbon?

The man and his group had not taken anything from the camp, as near as she had been able to tell, so the strange arti-fact would not be discovered. If it had been, she'd be able to deflect them by suggesting perhaps that it had been an aircraft part.

Nobody could ever know that it might have come off of a crashed spaceship.

Zareen stayed curled up against Ghada for warmth, noting the rage that seemed to power her friend and body-guard now, even greater than Ghada's embarrassment that they had been captured.

Zareen doubted that Ghada would ever sleep again, if they got out of this mess, unless Zareen went back to the highlands of Persia to recruit another few young women trained in the ancient ways of combat by the secret masters.

Although, truth be told, having a small army of such women around might make Zareen's missions safer, as well as more interesting. It was a man's world, yet.

Finn Severijns generally kept his comments to himself, even if his eyes were perhaps more forward than acceptable in English society. Hans Fertig had only needed to be rebuffed the once and seemed content that Zareen did not desire his companionship.

Most men would not see a handful of women as a threat, wrapped up in their chauvinistic fantasies.

Yes, having a group of women warriors might be a lovely idea, especially if the Frenchman and his gang of killers had finally decided to pursue her so hard and relentlessly.

He might be a threat, certainly. At least to her life.

These tribesmen might yet be a threat to her virginity, but she hadn't figured out how she was going to work around that problem. Finn and Hans might object, but they were badly outnumbered and not trained in the combat arts like Ghada and her cousins.

The cold was bracing, but Zareen vowed to sleep in pants and a better shirt in the future. She had let her guard down, convinced that the two pilots were not a threat.

They indeed had not been, but that had not meant she was safe.

Hopefully she would be able to learn from this experience. Certainly, the men did not change into anything delicate and cold to sleep.

Why should women?

They drove on through the night, hugging the outer edge of Gabal El Uweinat's western face, surrounded by silent tribesmen on horseback.

Eventually, the truck slowed, groaning like a dying beast as it coasted to a stop. Quickly, the leader and his riders dismounted and handed off their horses to two men who led them off out of sight.

The three men who had ridden with them in the bed of the truck got out now, and there were more weapons pointed at her and the others than was perhaps polite, but there were no threats, as yet.

As yet.

The leader approached and gestured politely for them to climb down as well. Finn led, as he tended to do. Zareen felt Ghada wrap the quilt around Zareen's shoulders and help her to her feet, when Hans handed her down.

It was unseemly for Ghada to stand around in nothing but a simple shift, but a man approached with piles of cloth that the leader thrust into her hands.

"Dress," he ordered simply. "We will talk inside."

Zareen fumbled with the fabric, but it turned out to be a collection of several robes, and she was able to slip one over her head for now. On a man as tall as Finn or the Bedouin leader, it would only come down to their boot tops, most likely, but they clung to both her and Ghada's bare ankles.

They were led to a pile of sand that resolved itself into something like a bunker when she got close. An open door revealed a lit interior down three steps, and then farther back into the face of the mountain itself.

As Zareen got to the door itself, the spilling light revealed that it was a metal box that had been assembled in place, apparently with screws or rivets. The whole was perhaps twenty feet wide, with sand piled up against both sides and atop it as perhaps camouflage.

Finn ducked to enter and then went down the steps, where he was able to stand normally. Zareen followed, then Ghada and Hans, and even the big German mechanic was able to walk upright in here.

The interior reminded her of the old drawings of tents kept by Victorian soldiers on campaign, with a red and black rug dominating the floor. Several folding campaign chairs and a number of mismatched trunks lined the walls.

The air even smelled damp and heavy, but hadn't Hassanein found a number of previously unknown springs that allowed caravans in the interior?

What better place to build yourself a small, hidden outpost than atop a spring?

The leader sat them down in four chairs, and then took one himself, leaving half a dozen men standing around them with guns and knives.

"I am Emad al-Sadri," he introduced himself in English, speaking with a crisp, almost Kentish accent. "Who are you people, and what are you doing here?"

The name sounded familiar, but Zareen couldn't place it. Still, the man had learned English from an Englishman at some point, which suggested that he was at least reasonably educated. That, in turn, suggested him to be from an important family, possibly even related to the exiled Emir, Idris of Cyrenaica.

She could only hope. That would make her job easier.

"I'm Finn Severijns," the bluff American said simply, his tones betraying that Montana background in a manner that simply could not be faked, even by a credible actor. "This is Hans Fertig. That's our plane back there. *Cerberus.*"

"I see," al-Sadri said in a hostile tone. "You are working for the Italians, Mr. Severijns?"

"Hell, no," Finn started to rise in anger, but subsided when the various Bedouins pointed guns again. "What gave you that stupid idea?"

"Your aircraft," al-Sadri said. "The one with the large Italian flag on the tail. Perhaps you could explain that, then?"

It was odd to Zareen, watching and hearing that Kentish accent emerge from an Arab face. But then, she frequently did the same to others, now that she thought about it, even if her own accent was a much posher western London, occasionally interspersed with a touch of the Highlands picked up from trips to Edinburgh to visit her paternal grandmother, Olivia MacQuaid.

She watched Finn grumble under his breath for a moment, staring down at the floor long enough that she was afraid he wouldn't speak, before he suddenly looked up.

"Those bastards owe me a lot of money, al-Sadri," Finn said in a voice tinged with rough menace. Something she had not heard from the man in the few days since she had made his acquaintance. "I suppose that we're in territory the Italians claim right now, if the maps are accurate enough. Are you working for the Italians?"

Emad al-Sadri reacted almost as though he'd been slapped as Zareen watched. His eyes blinked and his jaw came up.

Thank God that the other Bedouins in the room didn't speak English, or Zareen would have worried that one of them would have shot Finn for that. But she didn't suppose the American had that great an understanding of the various conflicts that had roiled Tripolitania, Fezzan, and Cyrenaica since the Italians went to war with the Ottomans in 1911 over these various territories.

A dull, ugly silence hung over the room for a moment before the Bedouin man suddenly laughed.

"American, yes?" he asked, in a much lighter tone than Zareen had expected.

"That's right," Finn answered as Zareen held her breath.

"Why do you hate the Italians so much, Severijns?" al-Sadri asked easily.

"I had been hired to fly for one of their airlines," Finn said, still a little peevishly. "Did you bother reading the Aurora Italia Airlines painted under that stupid flag?"

"I did not," al-Sadri answered in a soft voice. "But I am willing to grant you that much for now. We can always prove you a liar tomorrow if need be."

Finn didn't seem to catch the implicit threat behind those words, but he wasn't Arab, nor had he spent much time around them as far as she knew, other than to pick up the usual basics of language.

"Fine. Whatever," Finn continued. "So we were flying a group of folks from Rome to Abyssinia on this most recent run. Some to Gondar, some to Addis Ababa. Got as far as Cairo when we found out that the company had been shut down. Some jackass in Rome had cabled the Cairo office and fired everyone on the spot. Same for the others, from what I've heard. That left Hans and me stranded and unemployed in Egypt, out our last paycheck. Everything."

"And the aircraft?" al-Sadri asked, turning more sober, but not more serious, as far as Zareen could tell from watching the man. "The Ford Trimotor you call *Cerberus*?"

"Honestly?" Finn asked, also less belligerent now.

Emad al-Sadri nodded.

"I stole the damned thing," Finn admitted. "Happy?"

Zareen had suspected, but been unable to prove without asking the wrong sorts of questions.

The kind that might have brought the British Army authorities down to have a chat with the man she had wanted to hire.

Emad al-Sadri smiled now.

"You stole the aircraft from the Italians?" he asked.

"Yeah," Finn agreed. "I suppose that their government probably owns it, technically, depending on who might have bought things out of a bankruptcy court when the company was shut down. They want it, they can damned well come get it from me, but I'm willing to argue with them in an Egyptian court, at least if I can get it back to Egypt in one piece. Anything to stick a finger in somebody's eye over this."

She could almost see the waves of anger rising off Finn's head. The rumors had suggested many things. Fortunately, they had been largely accurate.

She smiled.

al-Sadri also laughed.

"It is likely that you will not have to face an Italian judge as a result of meeting me, Severijns," the Bedouin said. "Perhaps other things, but not that."

"So who are you people?" Finn asked, more curious than bellicose.

"In good time, my friend," al-Sadri replied in a lighter tone.

He turned to stare at her now.

Bright eyes in a face naturally dark and then tanned and lined by the sun. She concealed a start when she realized that the man had blue eyes, rather like Finn's or Hans's. She had been expecting dark pools like her own.

"So I am satisfied that these two are close enough to what they appear," al-Sadri said to her in a careful voice, almost a barrister challenging a witness's memory. He gestured to Ghada with one hand. "And I am reasonably confident that this woman is your maid and perhaps guardian. Who are you, mistress?"

Again, the confusing mismatch of an Arab face and a Kentish accent. The blue eyes didn't help her composure.

"Zareen Shirazi," she answered simply.

Any lies she gave him on something so simple could be easily disproven. All he would have to do was get into her papers.

"You are English, but not," al-Sadri said. "Even my accent is acquired, but yours is native, as are your mannerisms. And Shirazi is not an English name."

"My father is Anglo-Scottish," Zareen said carefully. "My mother is Persian. Their romance fell somewhere between the joys of *Cinderella* and the tragedy of *Romeo and Juliet*. They could not marry, but the tribal elders also recognized the simple truth of my existence, so allowed me to be raised in both places. Neither parent ever married."

He nodded, perhaps more acutely aware of someone forced to live in two different worlds by choices made by their parents.

Or society's unwelcoming conservatism in the face of two people in love.

"Mistress Shirazi, what brings you to Gabal El Uweinat?" he asked.

She took a deep breath and stared at the man, wondering which cover story she needed to tell him.

How many layers of misdirection and innuendo did she need to employ?

"Before I tell you, I must ask a question," she countered, waiting for him to nod before she proceeded. "Are you Senussi? Or Italian?"

Apparently, the Arabic men around the room understood those two words. Maybe nothing more, but the latter got a growl of distaste.

"The Italians have killed many of my cousins," al-Sadri said. "Nearly all of them. Most of the rest are in camps on the coast, where they may and may not continue to live, depending on that fat bastard in Rome and his whims. The Brotherhood resists as well as we can. My men and I ambush Italian patrols from the north and French ones from the southwest. We raid camps outsiders seek to establish, trying to control every oasis possible. Because you are English and American, you are not automatically my enemy. Does that help?"

"It does, Emad al-Sadri," Zareen nodded, letting her voice grow calm and serious. "The world knows me as an amateur archaeologist. I am, however, following a rumor of an experimental aircraft that crashed somewhere inside Gabal El Uweinat. A German aircraft, far from where it should be, possibly part of the Italian campaign in Abyssinia."

Dead silence fell on the small room. The men standing around grew a little restless, but al-Sadri was perfectly still.

"Are you a spy, Shirazi?" he finally asked in a voice like chipping flakes off of a flint arrowhead.

"I am not at liberty to discuss that, al-Sadri," Zareen replied tartly. "For reasons that should probably be obvious."

Finn had turned to stare at her, his face turning white. She was able to read his lips, but he didn't actually speak the profanity out loud in the presence of ladies, thankfully.

"There is a war coming, al-Sadri," she continued. "I

suspect that it will spill over into Cyrenaica almost immediately, given the personalities and geography involved."

"So you think we should help you?" he challenged her.

"An hour ago, I didn't even know you existed," she volleyed right back into his lap. "I hired Finn and Hans to transport us here so we could look. In Cairo, my fascist enemies are no doubt awaiting me with sharpened knives, but they don't know where I intended to go, and nobody was able to follow Finn's expert flying that got us here. I would personally be happy to go back and finish my work in the basin and be gone in a few days, never to return."

Something about her words caused the man to grow serious, but Zareen wasn't sure what she had said. Or rather, which part.

Most of it had been reasonable lies, almost impossible to disprove in the current circumstances. She was just sorry that she'd been forced to drag Finn and Hans into it, as they would have to have a long chat with some chipper gentlemen back in Cairo in another week.

Then they would have to make some hard decisions. Especially Hans, as he was a German, and those were the folks most likely to start the trouble next time. If he wasn't loyal to the new regime, he might have to flee to a neutral third nation until the future became evident.

Finn, she trusted. He wore his emotions and his loyalties largely on his sleeve.

Emad al-Sadri would be a different problem. He wasn't supposed to be this far south or east, if she remembered a briefing at the English embassy in Lisbon, right before she left. And if he was the man she had been told about.

She was obviously inside a hidden base from which he

could strike easily in any direction, retiring into the desert ahead of pursuit. At least pursuit that didn't have aircraft.

Modern technology was likely to completely upend desert warfare, when trucks equipped with enough fuel could cross the desert without watering holes, to say nothing of aircraft like *Cerberus*.

How would Emad al-Sadri react to the future intruding on his world?

He studied her with a complex series of emotions on his face. Worse than Finn, but the American was a genial, friendly sort to begin with. And Hans might fool most people with his gruff silence, but she'd caught the little jokes passing back and forth between the men.

"I think that you will stay here tonight," al-Sadri announced. "As my guests, however involuntary it might be. In the morning, we will talk again, and perhaps visit your camp to explore your tale for veracity. Then we will determine what is to happen next."

She couldn't help but shudder at the implications. It was possible that he could become a useful ally, especially if he represented a large band of Senussi warriors fighting the Italians.

However, he also might decide to simply kill her and the others to protect his own secrets.

He rose abruptly and gestured his men outside a closed door, where someone was no doubt guarding them. It wasn't like she could run far, since neither she nor Ghada had shoes. Nor would there be any around that would fit.

"Now what?" Finn asked, looking around.

"Now, we wait," Zareen replied.

"Are they likely to kill us?" Hans broke his usual silence.

"That remains to be seen."

CHAPTER TWENTY-ONE

He'd maybe slept. Mostly dozed. Finn couldn't get himself relaxed enough.

Didn't help that the Arab expected him to sleep on the wooden floor, barely muffled by a throw rug and a few blankets that they'd found in one of the trunks.

Finn had ended up leaning back against a trunk with a blanket behind him. It let him get comfortable enough. They had been left some kerosene lamps, which they had turned down to dimness.

Hans snored like usual, but he slept on the floor of *Cerberus* most nights anyway. This would be nothing new for him.

Zareen Shirazi didn't snore so much as purr loudly in her sleep. Finn grinned at the image of her as a big kitten. Maybe a mountain lion kitten. He had no doubt that the young woman was more dangerous than she appeared.

That Mauser wasn't for the meek or faint of heart.

Ghada had taken up a position seated cross-legged in a lotus across from him. She looked like one of those weird

Buddha statues he'd come across occasionally, serenely studying the world.

If them Arab boys were set to cause trouble, no doubt Ghada would be more than they could handle. And Finn already knew he was going to hell, according to all the good folks back home, so maybe he'd have to bring a few desert tribesmen with him.

He checked his watch. Wound it, just because. It kept pretty good time, most days, so he presumed that the sun was just coming up outside.

Morning prayers facing northeast from here, and then there was like to be a mite of trouble brewing.

Finn rose and stretched. Might as well be limber when they came, in case he needed to go down fighting.

Ghada did, too, except that she started doing some strange dance in slow motion while he watched, utterly fascinated. She had a second robe over the first, but he'd seen damned near everything last night, anyway.

Now, she was stepping just so and waving her hands in something that looked a little Chinese and a little Pacific Islander Hula.

Right until he realized that at high speed, he'd just watched her punch one man, pivot to block a second, strike a third, and kick a fourth.

Oh, shit.

It looked so much more friendly and pretty dialed all the way down to this speed.

Who the hell were these women?

Zareen was some sort of Persian princess, maybe? She sure as hell wasn't a peasant woman, to have been sent to England regularly to visit her father's side of the family. Or to have a killer as a maid when she did.

At least Ghada smiled at him as she worked.

Finn didn't like being in over his head, but it wasn't like it was anything alien at this point in his life, either.

A key entered the lock on the door rather noisily. Finn stepped over and tapped Hans with his foot to wake the man, while Ghada did the same with Zareen.

The door opened a moment later and Finn turned to find out his fate.

al-Sadri entered first. No, check that. Alone.

Seriously?

"Good, you are all awake," the man said with a smile. "After breakfast I have what I think will be a pleasant challenge for you this morning."

Finn nodded to the man as Hans grumbled and stood up. Which he did every morning.

Weirdly, the Bedouin was carrying what looked like women's sandals in one hand. Handmade, maybe, but a solid bottom and leather straps to go over the foot and up the ankle. He handed them to Ghada and Zareen, then stood back while the woman put them on.

Seriously not the way Finn expected his morning to go, but he wasn't going to look a gift horse in the mouth right now.

"Come," the man said, leading them back up the stairs and outside.

They were tight up against the western edge of the slope, and Finn could see other boxes like this one, carefully hidden to the point you might be able to drive along the valley headed south and miss them entirely if you didn't know they were there.

al-Sadri led them to the entry of a box canyon that surprised the hell out of him. Past the narrow mouth of the wadi, it opened out pretty quickly to show what his brain kept wanting to interpret as a small army camp, with tents and semi-permanent buildings along the edges and hidden so well with netting and such overhead that he was pretty sure he could have flown right over them at low altitude, knowing what to look for, and missed it.

Might have yesterday.

There was even a corral filled with some prime horseflesh and several watering troughs.

Almost felt like home. Especially the ripe smell of manure.

The men in here stared at the two women and largely ignored him and Hans, but he wasn't offended. Probably the first women they'd ever seen in here.

Everything went well for now. They went into a tent with a couple of trestle tables and were served what tasted like oatmeal flavored with some sweet spices, along with a warm tea that was welcome after the cool air around them.

It would get much warmer today.

When they were done eating, al-Sadri led them to a big tent that had been erected over a truck of some sort.

Only when he got close did Finn recognize the damned thing.

How the hell had they stolen an Italian armored car? Or driven it all the way out here?

He'd been shanghaied last night in an old Ford flatbed, so it was apparently possible to drive this far. You'd need a lot of fuel to do it, but Finn didn't figure that there was much out there that could argue with a damned mobile pillbox.

He looked up as he got under the pavilion hiding them from the sun and prying eyes. Sure enough, Lancia 1ZM armored car. The old 1918 model, with only the one big turret on top, rather than the second one atop that. And those rails on the front for cutting wire.

Old Lancia civilian truck, modified with armor. Krauts were doing more interesting things, last he'd heard, putting cannons on small armored cars as well as building faster tanks than the lumbering beasts he'd flown over during the Great War.

But twin 8mm machine guns would do just fine against men on horses in the desert, where the only cover that they might find would be the rolling terrain. No forests around here to hide in.

Finn turned to Hans and they shared a silent joke about Italians. Must have been one hell of a funny story about how this thing had gotten stolen.

al-Sadri stopped and turned to them, his face all serious now.

"I am willing to make you a trade, Finn Severijns," he said. "My men are Bedouins, and do not have the knowledge of how to fix this thing, so we towed it here, lest a patrol find it and recover it. But if we could take it into battle, it would radically change the balance of power in the desert."

Finn grinned. Yeah, he could see that. Thick walls in a village might stop those bullets, and they might not. But they'd sure do a fine job of keeping the Italians bottled up until they had to surrender when they ran out of food and water.

And if you caught a truck convoy in the open desert, you'd be able to go all pirate on them.

He'd heard some of the things the Italians were doing in Africa, but at the time he'd been more interested in having a steady job. World was still just coming out of the Great

Depression a decade later, and there were always more men than jobs.

Finn turned to Hans and caught a mild shrug. Thing was less complicated than *Cerberus*, and not American made, so something minor had probably broken in the engine somewhere. Quality Italian craftsmanship, and all that, where *pretty* was far more important than *reliable*.

Kinda like the company that had stranded his ass in Cairo in the first place. Pretty paint job, unreliable bastards in charge.

"Trade?" he asked al-Sadri.

"If you can fix it, we will extract a promise of silence from you about our base here and trust you to honor it after you leave."

"Might not be repairable, ya know," Finn explained. "Or maybe we end up jerry-rigging something for now but it breaks again. Might need a full machine shop to fabricate parts. Or maybe sneak into someplace and steal what you need."

"I understand," al-Sadri said. "For you, I ask you to take a look and let us know what can be done. While you do that, I will escort the women back to your camp where they can get dressed properly and we can talk about their archaeological undertaking."

Finn didn't like the sound of that, but there wasn't much he could do without causing more trouble. And the guy had been a pretty good gentleman about things, when it could have gone much worse.

He caught Ghada's eye and the shadow of a nod, and that made him feel better. That woman was way larger trouble than she looked at first glance. Those knives she carried around with her all the time made more sense now, since she might just be able to kill several men with them, especially if she surprised them.

And she would.

Zareen also nodded calmly, like she could read his mind or something.

"We'll do what we can," Finn promised the man.

Not much more that he could say.

CHAPTER TWENTY-TWO

Zareen had not been sure what this stranger was about, but he produced two pairs of loose pants for her and Ghada, allowing them to ride, rather than relegating them to the truck as mere passengers. It was uncomfortable, to be sure, using stirrups with sandals rather than boots like the men had, but they had also been given relatively docile horses to ride.

Emad al-Sadri led the small caravan, with her beside him and Ghada on her other side. A dozen or so men were strung out behind them in two columns, all heavily armed with rifles and swords that she had missed last night.

This was the high desert. Gilf Kebir. *The Great Barrier* that separated the Nile Valley from the lands of Fezzan and Cyrenaica. One of the driest places on Earth, supposedly.

They rode slowly at first, but once al-Sadri recognized that she and Ghada were competent riders, they sped up until they moved at a hard canter. You could do that with well-watered and fed horses, so the man must have some sort of supply chain. Zareen simply had no idea how far the friendships of the vast Senussi Brotherhood might reach.

The movement itself was Sufi in origin, going back perhaps a century, but rather than swear a life of poverty and alms, members were expected to work in their villages to support themselves. Rather than embrace the ecstatic, as she understood it, the elders preached a sober thoughtfulness that meant to split the difference between the dancers and adherence to the rigid scholars.

But for the Italians, Emir Idris of Cyrenaica might be a king of all Libya now, presiding over a modernizing, powerful country, just as Egypt next door was slowly coming into the twentieth century after so many generations of backwardness under the Ottomans and others before them.

"What will you do when the war comes?" Zareen asked al-Sadri in a voice that only he could hear.

"Your war," he replied, glancing over. "My war began more than twenty-five years ago."

"*The War*," she offered. "The one everyone expects is coming. The conflagration that will engulf us all."

"My Emir is already secretly an ally of the English," al-Sadri said. "Quietly, they have assisted us against the Italians. If the greater war does come, I would expect the frontier to become a battlefield, and we will finally have allies that can openly help us push the Italians back into the sea. That we can be our own country, and not some lapdog colony of others."

Zareen let the conversation lapse as she ruminated on a reply.

The man could be an ally, but only in her missions for the English. She dared not let him find out too much about the alien wreckage she had found. It would not hold up as a

German aircraft, if she was able to find larger pieces under that rubble.

At the same time, there would not be an easy way to slip in here and dig, unless she brought the man completely into the conspiracy.

Even the British government had no idea of the true depths of the things she had discovered already. They were all more concerned that the Germans or the Japanese would somehow be able to tap the metaphysical and produce a weapon or advantage that would let them quickly conquer the world.

They believed that they held the edge in the technological.

However, it would not take much to knock out the French and the Polish. The Russians were an unknown, inwardly facing power, even worse than the Americans.

Only Britain stood in a position to stop the fascists from conquering the entire world. The English might be racist, classist prigs of the worst sort, and she had personally experienced some of their ugliest parts in the upper-class salons, but they also were firmly wedded to the belief in honest rules that applied to everyone. In the fair shake.

The Americans rivaled them in that, a cultural heritage that bound them into a greater whole.

Zareen would need the British, even as badly as they constantly meddled in Persia, if she wanted to free her true home from the control of outsiders, just as Emad al-Sadri did.

"Where did you learn English?" she asked, dancing carefully sidelong into her deeper question.

The man turned his head to fully study her.

"My father, like yours, was an outsider," he finally said. "As you no doubt can tell from my eyes."

Zareen nodded, aware of the number of times she had also had to explain her mixed heritage to people with curiosity ranging from idle to hostile.

"But the Grand Senussi ruled that I be raised as a cousin of the family that I was," al-Sadri continued. "He is not bound by the old ways that have failed us so badly, and instead saw a future where the Senussi Brotherhood expanded to the entire Maghreb, and perhaps the whole Islamic *Ulama*, bringing a modernizing conservatism that could strike a balance."

Cousin of the Grand Senussi?

Emad al-Sadri looked to be roughly thirty years old, if she had to guess. In that case, the man who had been the *Grand Senussi* when Emad al-Sadri had been born had married one of his daughters to Emir Idris.

Emad al-Sadri would thus be Senussi royalty, or whatever the correct term would be, on a distaff branch. Easily raised in a palace somewhere, and educated as broadly as the Senussi Brotherhood believed in.

Rather like a Persian princess from a poor, Highland family.

Interesting.

Especially considering how many Senussis and other Libyans the Italians had killed in their various campaigns in the last generation.

"And you are not working with the British Military, Miss Shirazi," al-Sadri said after a moment. "They would have warned me you were coming and sent you with a letter of introduction."

"My relationship with the British government at Whitehall is informal at best, and secret," Zareen replied. "I do not have direct dealings with the Army, and this particular operation was not something many people knew about."

"And yet, your enemies await you in Cairo?" he pressed.

"A Frenchman," she said. "An industrialist with fascist leanings who seeks to steal inventions and advanced technology, wherever he might find it, and turn it into weapons that he will use to overthrow the Republic and no doubt institute a fascist government modeled after his two heroes."

"I am unaware of any German aircraft crashing in this area in the recent past," al-Sadri glared at her.

"We pursue rumors, sir," Zareen replied, trying not to sound evasive with her lies. "Not all of them turn into truths. If I was sure of myself, we would have brought a larger expedition. I needed to prove one way or the other that there was a reason to do so."

More than that would be unsafe to share. In the distance, she could already see the reflection of light off *Cerberus* and the dark spot in the sand where her tent had been set last night.

Hopefully, any tracks had been blown away or overridden by horses, and nobody had actually watched them digging yesterday. Perhaps the sound of the aircraft had been all they had known, and then had spent the afternoon scouring the sands for intruders.

With luck, her secrets yet persisted.

CHAPTER TWENTY-THREE

It was an absolute pain in the ass, Finn decided, trying to communicate with people who didn't speak any English, once the boss guy had left. He knew enough Arabic to get by, but he doubted that even the technical terms would have helped.

He was dealing with boys fresh off the farm, like he'd been twenty years ago, volunteering to go fight the Krauts overseas.

At least someone had liberated a pretty good toolkit when they stole the armored truck.

Hans had gotten the truck's engine compartment open and poked around for a bit, looking for anything obviously broken. He looked up and shook his head.

"Turn it over," he said.

Finn nodded. Hans was in charge when it came to fixing things, just like Finn did most of the flying. That was the secret that made them such a great team.

Finn started to move to the driver's door, but the boys in

here got twitchy. Fingers found triggers, but nobody said anything.

Still, better safe than sorry.

Finn pointed at the one who looked the brightest in the batch.

"Driver?" he asked.

Pure confusion. Yeah, going to be that kind of day.

Finn held up his hands and mimicked holding a steering wheel, jiggling it back and forth for a second. The guy lit up at that and pointed at another man.

Oh, right, the guy who knew how to drive the Ford flatbed. Should have known.

Finn pointed at the man.

"You, start the engine," he said, gesturing the man to open the door and get in.

More confusion.

Finn made a sound like the starter turning over, feeling like a complete fool.

But it worked. The fellow lit up as well and jumped in, setting the choke, feeding it gas, and hitting the starter.

Or whatever you did in a stolen Italian armored truck.

Finn just flew Fords.

The engine turned over. Then it sputtered. Caught for just a moment, and then died again.

"Okay, good enough," Hans yelled over the noise.

Finn waved his hands at his new driver and got the guy to stop doing whatever he was up to.

"Got an idea?" Finn turned and called.

"Maybe," Hans called back. "Problems with the fuel line, or maybe the filter."

"Let me find you a blanket and we can move the tools around," Finn answered, looking around.

Not like he was going to be able to explain it in literary detail to these boys.

Still, they had stolen some good stuff. Almost worth stealing himself, to use on *Cerberus*, but that was probably an even dumber idea than it sounded. He found a tarp to lay underneath and got it in place, running around the damned truck several times to pull it flat, not trusting the boys to understand.

He really needed to learn more Arabic if he was going to keep hanging out with Zareen and Ghada. That was certain.

They went to work, Hans settled on his back underneath, with Finn kneeling next to him with the toolbox handy.

He just tried to ignore all the guns that were vaguely pointed in his direction.

CHAPTER TWENTY-FOUR

Asher had friends in the slums.

Far more than most people could probably imagine, because he literally could never forget a face or a voice, to say nothing of a favor.

And the Egyptians took favors more seriously than even the Durren.

More than once, he had to turn down offers of food or tea as hospitality. He could not consume any of it, but that was the default position with the locals when they saw him.

He had not acquired a reputation as a wizard, for which he thanked whatever human gods might be watching over him, but as a deep, analytical scholar. A man able to read any text written, and then parse it well enough to explain to illiterate Egyptian dockworkers who probably would have been lawyers and doctors in a fair and just society.

The people of the slums had adopted him as one of their own as a result.

Today, he felt like the European stories of a piper, leading mice away, but then he didn't get paid, so taking the children instead.

Around him, nearly a dozen of the brighter children that outsiders would deride as mere urchins.

Asher knew better.

Already he had formulated a plan to teach some of these children the skills and knowledge they would need as adults if they wished to break out of the class of their birth. It did not, as far as he could calculate, violate any of his programming to help uplift a small section of the Egyptian slums.

Working with the government in any sort of semi-official category would be a different story, but he could merely walk into the sea where no humans could follow if that became necessary.

Perhaps he would surface in South America and start over, in that case. Or a Pacific Island, far from prying eyes.

For today, he had called in a few favors. Asked these children's parents for help. Been nearly overwhelmed with the response, until he culled the group down to the dozen best suited to this task, while assigning less dangerous tasks to the rest.

He studied his pupils. Asher was tempted to call them his army, but that would suggest he was planning things that would violate his programming. Instead, he was upholding society against corrosive elements, and in doing so fulfilling his dictates, because without a proper society, there was nothing to study.

"You understand that you are merely to watch these men and track them for me, yes?" he asked.

Nods, a few more glumly from the older ones, the boys developing their pickpocket skills to prey on hapless foreigners.

"They are dangerous men," Asher said. "Killers who would simply shoot you in the street, rather than chasing after you. I will not have that on my conscience."

Or whatever an *Autonomous Simulated Human Exploration Robot* had for a conscience.

"I wish to know where they are staying," Asher repeated. "When they leave. When they return. Once we know their patterns, then we will consider doing something rude to them."

That got smiles. Already, these dozen boys, ranging from nine to thirteen, were aware that the two men at the heart of the conspiracy were foreigners. Not the hated British, but Frenchmen. Along with the Italians, the Frenchmen had a much worse reputation as colonial masters, all things considered, although that might be as difficult as telling a white and black thread apart at dawn, in order to call the morning prayers.

"Questions?" Asher asked, fearing that they might actually have some.

These dozen children were all better suited to moving in the slums of Cairo than he was, even with his much greater experience. They were human. They fit the cultural and biological matrix of this planet, while one robot was merely trying to remain as quietly hidden as possible.

Plus, actively committing crime was not something his programmers had ever envisioned. Most humans could be reduced to crime in order to feed their family, but Asher did not need food. He did not need a place to sleep, as he merely walked at night to update his cartographical and geographical maps of the city.

Fortunately, the children had no questions. He had chosen them for their savvy, setting the others merely to watching for the authorities to respond to his activities. Or his competitors, although even those tended to be friendly.

Old favors, as a thing, went bone-deep in this town.

"Then off with you," Asher instructed his tiny army. "I will pass this way at the agreed times and check in."

They scattered like a sirocco had entered the alley, gone every which way in an instant.

Asher considered what he had unleashed on the underworld of Cairo. His studies of humans suggested the possibility that these dozen children might turn into the nucleus of a political and social movement as they turned into adults.

Possibly a revolution.

It behooved him to make sure they were a positive impact.

The Durren would never forgive him for overturning human civilization.

CHAPTER TWENTY-FIVE

Zareen and Ghada had both been able to dismount their steeds before Emad got to them to help, and she saw the newly born respect in the man's eyes.

Too used to dealing with Arabic women who were kept confined, rather than Persian and English, who could see to their own needs.

The sun was not yet high, but it would be a hot day. The horses were moved to the far side of *Cerberus* for now, standing in the shade of the plane away from Finn's hammock.

"Ladies, would you care to change?" Emad asked gallantly, gesturing towards the tent.

"Should I wear my Mauser pistol, or leave it in the trunk until later?" Zareen asked.

He had been a gentleman up until now. She didn't see that necessarily changing, but the women having guns would alter the equation significantly, from prisoner/jailer to fellow travelers.

The man studied her closely, seeking something in her eyes.

Zareen stood proud, shoulders back and head up, tilted just enough to convey her strength and conviction to the man.

"Are you a threat?" he asked obliquely.

"Are you?" Zareen countered.

He surprised her by laughing.

"Indeed not, Lady Shirazi," he said. "Go. I will tell my men."

Zareen felt a little deflated, but turned and walked into the tent with Ghada right behind her.

"How dangerous are these men?" Ghada asked quietly once the tent flap was down.

Rather than immediately undressing, the woman grabbed her two knives and stood watch for her mistress.

"I think we would have already seen the bad side of them, if that was what Emad had planned," Zareen decided, removing her sandals and starting to pull the outer robe over her head.

She saw the piece of the alien spacecraft resting on a small, folding table where she had left it last night. As she opened the trunk for her clothes, it went in deep, where it would hopefully remain hidden for the time being.

The rest of the tent was as she had left it. Even the man being punched had not disturbed anything, as he had collapsed bonelessly to the ground.

Quickly, she stripped nude and began to dress, the various layers an English adventuress required in the hot desert. Last was the Mauser, hanging in a leather holster that went over her shoulder like the traveling bag she slung opposite it.

With the kepi in place, she was prepared. Only then did Ghada strip, quickly shifting things around until not much had changed, other than everything fit and her robes contained a wealth of hidden pouches and gear the woman traveled with at all times.

Zareen emerged first, followed by Ghada, a white ghost in her wake.

Emad looked up from what he was doing and the surprise on his face was honest. But then, he had only ever seen her as a victim. Not a player.

The men stirred uneasily, but nobody reached for a weapon.

"Certainly, you men cannot be afraid of a mere woman, can you?" she asked in a sweet, almost taunting, Arabic that probably reminded them of their mothers in a kitchen somewhere.

Hers had taught her that.

And it also put the men on a different footing. This was no mere woman, but a noble lady, English to boot. A peer of their leader, not prey for them to pursue.

She watched that lesson worm its way into these men like a wasp laying eggs. It brought a smile to her face.

Emad rose and closed the book he had been reading, slipping it into a pocket on his robes she hadn't noticed before.

"A great improvement, ladies," he smiled and bowed deeply to both of them. "Now, what do we know about crashed German aircraft?"

Zareen smiled, having thought about almost nothing for the last several hours except what she would tell this man.

It helped that he was a natural enemy of the Italians, and by extension, their German allies. And that he was possibly working with the British Army.

Hopefully, her lies would not be caught out easily.

"I was unable to acquire a Geiger counter," she began, referring to the interesting device the German physicist had been able to make portable enough to work in the field.

The threat of radiation might be sufficient to keep most of these men at a safe distance. And it was only a shade of evil to imply, on her part.

"You expect dangerous radiations?" Emad asked, surprising her.

A Senussi leader of a desert warband should not be that well educated. But hadn't he been reading while she dressed?

"It is a possibility not to be ignored," Zareen said. "As I said, experimental. The Austrian, Einstein, has revolutionized our understanding of the universe, and both Curie and Bohrs have extended that in different directions."

"Agreed," Emad nodded. "I would expect an atomic pile to be much too heavy for an aircraft, but perhaps the Germans are further advanced than anybody knows."

Zareen chided herself internally. This man was smart. And broadly educated, obviously. And rather handsome in a way she found more distracting than she preferred.

"Just so," she replied to cover her sudden fluster. "That being said, we had only just begun to quarter and explore this area..."

She paused, as Emad was staring over her shoulder, focused intently on something.

"What is it?" she asked.

She was surprised when he stepped closer than was proper, then turned her by her elbow. One hand went out and pointed, unfortunately at the exact spot where she had been digging yesterday.

"The wall is marred there, as though by an impact," he

explained. "Normally, the face would be equally weathered, but this has the look of new stone."

Zareen glanced over and realized the man was close enough to kiss her, if he felt adventurous enough to deal with Ghada later.

She decided to play along with the man's discovery, wondering if this was a test. Had someone seen them working yesterday and reported it?

"We noted the same," she replied. "However, all we have done to date is examine the surface."

"Shall we?" he asked, gesturing for several of the men to accompany him.

She noted that only about half did, with the others guarding the horses and the airplane.

Zareen fell in beside the man as he walked.

"If it struck the wall that hard, would you expect anything to survive meaningfully?" he asked, now treating her like an archaeologist and a scientist.

That was so far out of character for a Bedouin leader that she nearly forgot who he was as she talked.

"That is exactly why I wished to examine it," she replied. "One never knows when some scientist may have made a significant breakthrough and neglected to tell the scientific world in general about it."

Quickly enough, the little troop was standing before the pile where she had recovered the window that should not have survived such an impact. Zareen presumed that she had been being watched and adjusted her lies on the fly.

"Yesterday, we saw the same thing you did, and explored here for a time, but as you can see, these stones are far too great for us to remove, short of a major expedition where we literally undermine them and roll them off to one side," she said, gesturing.

The sands were already starting to fill in where she and the men had dug yesterday. In another day or two it would be as though nobody had ever been here.

"And you have explored no farther?" Emad asked, kneeling and peering into that gap where the glass had been uncovered, however briefly.

"We have not," Zareen could answer honestly. "*Cerberus* arrived a little after local noon, and we worked until perhaps dinner time."

He rose and smiled at her.

"Perhaps I can be of assistance, then," Emad said. "My men need to explore this series of canyons better than we have before, previously content to merely make sure nobody was hiding in here, but no more. Come."

They walked back to *Cerberus* and the man gathered his dozen warriors together.

"I will remain here with the ladies," he told them in Arabic as she stood mutely and listened. "You will explore in pairs, heading every direction to look for evidence of an aircraft crash. Return here at noon."

And with that, they were alone, just the three of them and their horses, tied up in the shade.

Ghada went domestic, surprising Zareen. Tea was brewed. A small table and three folding chairs were pulled from the travel trunk so the group could sit in the shade of the plane and just chat, like this was a salon in London or Edinburgh.

"So," Emad asked suddenly, sipping his tea. "Without my superstitious Bedouins around, what are you really up to?"

His smile was honest, suggesting that he understood her game to be far deeper than she had let on.

"You would not believe me," Zareen said after a moment to gather her wits back up.

Beside them, Ghada had come to a stillness so complete that Emad should have grown concerned, had he understood.

"Try me," the man said, also growing serious.

"You would think me mad," she tried a new tack.

"An Englishwoman, alone in the desert but for a bodyguard and a pair of hirelings to fly you around?" he asked with a hint of sarcasm. "Yes, most would."

Most?

"And you do not?" Zareen countered.

"We are all, to some extent, mad," he offered. "But you do not strike me as dangerously unbalanced. What truly brought you here?"

There. No other choice. She had to gamble.

"A crash," she said. He started to scoff but she overrode him, aware that she would need this man's help to even leave again. "Older than we expected."

"How old?" Emad's eyes got narrow.

"Perhaps during the Great War," she said. "Other clues suggest that as a timeline to explore."

"Nobody had an aircraft heavy enough to damage that wall sufficiently," he said, gesturing almost angrily. "It would have taken a bomb, and that would have left burn marks. Other evidence."

"Do you really wish to know the truth, Emad al-Sadri?" Zareen felt her voice grow cold and hard.

He nodded warily now, aware that something had just changed around them.

"The thing that I seek was not an aircraft," she said simply.

"What was it, then?"

"A spacecraft," she explained.

"Truly?" he seemed properly astonished now.

"Some tribes tell of a brilliant light that lit up the very night as though day," she continued. "They didn't use a western calendar, so we think it was roughly 1916. The sound that followed was sharp but there was no earthquake felt. Later, witnesses claim they saw a skeleton walking across the desert, too skinny to be a man and unhindered by the sun and heat. Plus, it appeared to them as silvery white."

"Nobody has mentioned this to me," Emad breathed.

"You are from the north," Zareen smiled. "The tribes who saw it fled south, seeking refuge in the Wadai Empire when the Italians began to push into their territory. From there, the story crossed the Sahara to the Atlantic coast with the French. A Portuguese scholar heard bits and pieces but discounted them because it did not impact on their territories. I heard it and knew."

"Knew?" Emad challenged.

"There is a man in Cairo that I think is the visitor whose ship crashed here," Zareen said.

"Why did you not seek him out, then?" Emad asked.

It helped settle her that the man was treating this like a scholarly mission, rather than the ramblings of a crazed Englishwoman.

She'd wondered about herself more than once.

"Finding one man in the Cairo slums, if he does not wish to be found, would be impossible," Zareen said. "I hope to entice him to find me."

"Ah, by finding part of his ship or some other clue that he

could not ignore," the man nodded. "But why hide for so long? Would not others come to rescue him? Or should he contact some authority and make himself a power?"

"I do not know," Zareen shrugged. "Almost all of what I speak is pure supposition without factual evidence."

"Almost all?" he asked, catching the distinction.

"Crazed Englishwoman?" she asked.

"Doubtful," he replied. "Although I have no hesitation that you could fabricate such a role, if necessity demanded it. What did you find?"

He said it with such certainty, such conviction that Zareen knew she could not prevaricate her way out of this. She did not bother trying.

Instead, Zareen rose, resting her tea on the little table and moving to the tent. Inside, she located the piece of wreckage and again weighed it in her hand, thinking it to be made of feathers rather than the metal and glass it appeared.

She took a deep breath and emerged from the tent.

Emad studied her as she approached, eyes narrow.

Zareen placed the piece into his hands and sat down again, drinking her tea as though nothing whatsoever had happened in the world.

Emad turned the thing over his hands, making unconscious noises of wonder. He even went so far as to rap it gently with his knuckles, and then harder.

Finally he held it up to her like some magical talisman that would keep monsters at bay.

His mouth opened, but no sounds came out, let alone coherent thoughts.

"Something impacted that cliff face hard enough to fragment it," Zareen said, pointing at the object.

"What is this made of?" he finally managed.

"I have no idea," she answered him. "When I get back to a lab, I suspect I will not be any closer to an idea of what this is."

"Spaceship?" he asked again.

"Do you know anyone on Earth that could produce that metal or that glass?" she challenged him, perhaps a shade sharper than she should, but Zareen felt like making her point definitively.

"No," he admitted. "Outside of a fanciful story in a magazine, there is nothing. And I suspect that the Germans and the French and everyone else would kill for that knowledge."

"And probably the British as well," she nodded. "However, if the next Great War is indeed coming, we'll need something like this to stop the Germans and the Italians from overrunning everything."

The man fell silent, having some internal conversation to which she was not privy.

Finally he looked up at her. Then handed her the part when he started and realized he still held it.

"All of this is technically part of Cyrenaica," he gestured to the walls around them. "And by extension it will be an Italian colony under their laws."

"Which is why I came here from Cairo and not Tripoli, al-Sadri," she replied. "I do not feel that the world is better served with this sort of thing in Mussolini's hands."

"Agreed," he said. "However, hiding knowledge of this will be difficult. Even my men would talk if something were found out here, and that is likely to draw heavier Italian forces into the deep desert. Possibly even the French from the southwest, if they thought there was something valuable here."

"Then perhaps it would be best for now if we departed as soon as possible?" Zareen said. "I have enough, I think, to find the Man With No Face and entice him into talking, if he will."

"And your French adversary?" he asked.

"Perhaps it will finally be time to deal with the man directly, al-Sadri," she replied.

"Please, call me Emad," he said. "If we are to have a conspiracy of silence, it would be better to treat one another as friends."

"Emad," she nodded. "I am Zareen. And my assistant Ghada."

He shook both their hands in the western style, reminding her of nothing right now so much as how she imagined T.E. Lawrence must have looked before he died, helping the al-Saud revolt against the Ottomans during the Great War, on the way to proclaiming Sa'udi Arabian independence.

"Now, I think it would be for the best if we waited for my men to return, with whatever luck they have," Emad said. "But we will keep future patrols above ground, unless we find something so astonishing that it cannot be kept secret. As you said, better the British than the others."

"Indeed," Zareen nodded. She paused, looking for the right words. "What was it that you were reading earlier, Emad?"

She liked the blush that appeared. It made him look younger. Perhaps more innocent, as well.

"Kahlil," he answered, pulling out a small, leather-bound book in faded black and passing it to her.

It reminded her of a bible, the small ones with soft covers rather than a rigid hardcover.

Kahlil Gibran. It was a copy of ***The Prophet***, written in English rather than Arabic, which surprised her even more. Zareen was familiar with the man's work, but had never really spent much time reading it.

She read part of a page randomly opened now and realized how lyrical the words were:

> *Then, said Almitra, speak to us of*
> *love.*
> *And he raised his head and looked*
> *upon the people and there fell a*
> *stillness upon them. And in a*
> *great voice he said:*
> *When love beckons to you, follow him,*
> *Though his ways are hard and steep.*
> *And when his wings enfold you yield*
> *to him,*
> *Though the sword hidden among his*
> *pinions may wound you.*
> *And when he speaks to you believe*
> *in him,*
> *Though his voice may shatter your*
> *dreams as the north wind lays*
> *waste the garden.*

Zareen felt a blush creep up her own face as she handed the book back to the man.

Emad al-Sadri had not struck her as a romantic, but she supposed she had only seen the gruff military man, leading a band of soldiers in a campaign against the invaders of his beloved land.

"It brings me peace," he said simply, keeping the book in

hand. "But please, do not let me keep you from whatever work you need to do to record your excavations."

Zareen stared at him for a moment and then rose. A map of the immediate terrain would be useful. Later, she would have Finn fly overhead and she would take some pictures that she could use to get all the details correct.

She retreated to the tent as Ghada kept watch. Inside, she paused to consider how much of this she should actually commit to paper. If she was truly returning to Cairo, the man who had broken into her hotel room was likely to return. Her secrets needed to remain unwritten then.

Perhaps she should write a letter to Grandmother Olivia, instead, telling the woman about the strange six months she had just traversed. It would give her something useful to do and help frame everything more firmly in her memory, so that she didn't have to commit her crimes and suspicions to a page that might be intercepted.

Her life had become far more complicated than she had anticipated.

CHAPTER TWENTY-SIX

Finn wiped his hands with a clean-enough rag. It helped that they'd been working with gasoline, which was as good a solvent as anything.

Damned fuel filter hadn't probably been changed since the Great War was over, and the stupid thing had been nearly black when they got it out. Throw in a blockage behind it from all the crap that had accumulated in the fuel tank over time, and Finn was frankly amazed that they'd been able to start it at all.

Turned out, Omar was the driver. Finn had gotten that much, as tight-lipped as these boys tended to be. Omar was in the cab of the beast right now with Alawi, who seemed to be some kind of sergeant, if Finn had to make comparisons. Alawi seemed to be manning the big gun turret.

The starter growled, and then the engine caught. Hans had gone ahead and cleaned a decade's gunk off the spark plugs while he was at it, so the thing actually was almost as quiet and smooth as *Cerberus* on a bad day right now.

Wouldn't last, but that wasn't Finn's problem.

"Is good?" Omar yelled.

Hans slammed the hood down to latch it and waved.

"That's it," Finn yelled back. "You drive to test."

At least he hoped that was what he said. Hard to tell, but Omar dropped the thing into gear and lurched forward as everyone scrambled madly to get away from being run over.

He ended up next to Hans, down at one end of the line. They weren't really being guarded at this point, so several hours of male bonding over broken engines apparently transcended language and culture.

At least today.

In the distance, Finn picked up movement that resolved itself into a line of horsemen coming this way. And horsewomen, he hoped, acutely aware again that he and Hans were the only two around here without guns.

The boys around them also hopped more or less to as the stolen Italian warmachine rumbled out of the tent and began a wide circle, trailing a plume of black smoke that would hopefully get better as the engine ran a while.

The man in charge rode like a hero in a western movie back home. Tom Mix without the hat, maybe. Thank God the two women were with him, riding easily along. They'd even changed into what Finn was used to seeing them wearing.

And of course, he should have known that they were both expert riders, too.

Finn wondered if he should start making a list of the few things those two women *didn't* do. Likely shorter and easier. And would give them a checklist to knock things off of later.

Zareen was probably like that.

Finn and Hans were surrounded again by the time al-

Sadri rode up, escorted by the old Lancia 1ZM. He couldn't suppress the grin on his face, doubly so when the man approaching seemed to be in a good mood as well.

"I do not suppose that I could hire you?" he asked good-naturedly as he dismounted and shook hands with them.

The women did as well, and the boys around the outside of the circle relaxed, slinging rifles onto their backs for the first time all day.

"Pretty sure you couldn't afford my rates," Finn grinned back at the man. "How about you, Hans?"

"Need more dancing girls first," Hans said, eliciting a laugh from everyone who spoke English.

"Then I will need to recruit a mechanic," al-Sadri said in a sideways kind of way that got Finn to staring at him maybe a touch ruder than he should.

What are you up to, fellow?

al-Sadri turned until he could see all four of the outsiders in a half-circle.

"Zareen, I agree with you that there does not appear to be anything that can be done at present to formalize an excavation that might and might not find anything," he continued, speaking slowly enough that Finn realized he was talking to all the hard-ass Bedouins around him that might have a little English in them, despite not mentioning it all morning.

And we're on a first name basis now? What'd I miss?

"So I will happily send you on your way, as soon as you complete whatever preparation Finn and Hans need to do on *Cerberus*," al-Sadri continued. "However, when you return to Cairo, I'm coming with you."

Finn noted that the man was speaking directly to Zareen right now, ignoring the other three of them. He also watched her blink a little in surprise, apparently caught off guard by the pronouncement.

Finn figured it wasn't really his place to demand explanations about whatever had happened over there, but he was also still feeling a mite protective. Woman almost young enough to be his daughter, and all that, maybe being led astray by a handsome stranger who'd look damned good in a ten-gallon hat. White or black.

He caught her eyes now and waited for the significant, if tiny nod that said she was okay with it.

After all, if that fool was going aboard *Cerberus* by himself, he'd be outnumbered. And if Ghada was as dangerous as she'd looked this morning, Finn and Hans might not even have to get involved.

al-Sadri turned to Ghada now and caught her look of surprise that someone was asking her permission in all this. Like maybe she thought of herself as an extension of Zareen, which was stupid, however accurate it might be at times.

But Ghada nodded as well.

That left it up to him.

Finn caught the glances going around the circle as everyone turned to look at him now.

Damnit, Hans, not you, too. Fine.

"Don't think we can get everything done this afternoon and take off with enough time to get anywhere," Finn said. "But you should bring the truck over to *Cerberus* with you, al-Sadri."

"Call me Emad," he said. "Why is that?"

Oh, really?

"Emad," Finn nodded skittishly. "Because I've got seven barrels of fuel stashed inside. We'll need about six of them to refill the wing tanks, then I can leave the rest and the empties with you. Call it rent for borrowing your mountain for a few days.”

"Indeed, Severijns,” Emad said. “Thank you.”

"Call me Finn,” he said.

Sounded like the start of an adventure.

Or something equally stupid.

CHAPTER TWENTY-SEVEN

The airplane was an American invention, so Emad found it fitting that the first one he ever rode in was piloted by an American. And an ally, he hoped, but that remained to be seen.

The man had evinced a protective instinct around the women, so Emad had trod lightly. Except that it wasn't a wounded or thwarted lover beset by a romantic rival.

No, Finn, and to a lesser degree Hans, had both reacted like protective uncles to his presence, assuming the women would make their own decisions, but willing to step in if Emad al-Sadri overstepped any bounds.

Yes, that made sense. Bizarre, given how short the time this foursome had apparently been together, but Zareen Shirazi had that charisma about her, drawing complete strangers into her orbit.

Look at him.

Emad watched as Alawi supervised the loading of the last steel barrel into the bed of the truck, the one still nearly full, which would do much to expand their range for striking Italian targets.

It was morning, after a pleasant night among friends, both old and new. After writing messages and letters, leaving orders, and preparing his men for things they would need to do in his absence.

A messenger had been sent to Emad's superiors, farther southwest, informing them that he would be gone to Cairo, hopefully for only a few days, possibly returning with a competent mechanic who could keep the various vehicles repaired. And news of a new ally in the form of Zareen Shirazi, amateur explorer and archaeologist.

No mention anywhere of a crashed German experimental aircraft. That would just bring more strangers.

Finn Severijns walked close to Emad. Alone, as Hans was finishing other tasks.

"So we only brought the two seats," he seemed to be apologizing. "Left the rest in Cairo."

"I will be fine sitting on the floor, Finn," he said carefully, aware that their roles were very shortly about to reverse.

"Long as you're prepared," Finn nodded, returning to the aircraft and boarding now.

Emad glanced over and saw the women also preparing to enter the aircraft, separate if not that far away physically.

Emad saw an image of himself visiting Zareen's uncle at his palace, in the form of an American named Finn, arriving as an unknown stranger.

What were his intentions?

Even Emad wasn't sure at the moment. Certainly, she was beautiful, intelligent, and educated. What man would be able to resist such a combination?

However, she was also an outsider. English by culture

and upbringing, where he was a scion of the desert. Emad had never even left the rough boundaries of Cyrenaica, except for a few raids into Fezzan when the Italians weren't paying attention.

She had come to Egypt from Portugal. And France before that. And a myriad of exotic places he had only ever read about in his uncle's palace, before the Italians drove his families into exile.

She would not see Cairo as anything more than a way station headed elsewhere.

Dare he follow? Or ask her to return?

Emad knew no peace.

And he needed to go to Cairo. So many things depended on it. He could see that now, especially as the war everyone feared felt imminent. Italy would wish to pounce quickly on Egypt, perhaps catching the British unaware and stealing the colony so that they had an unbroken string of bases connecting the Italian peninsula to the Indian Ocean. If they controlled Suez, they might conquer the world.

Emad would die first. And take as many Italians as he could reach to hell with him.

He followed the rest aboard the aircraft, paying close attention to the process as Finn sealed the door behind him and gestured to a spot on the floor where several blankets had been set like a small nest.

Hans had moved the seats back a row, if Emad understood the process, once the barrels were emptied and offloaded. That left Emad near the front of the flying machine, where he could sit up and look out the side as they flew or place his back to the front wall and stare at Zareen.

It sounded like a pleasant way to spend several hours.

He took his spot.

Zareen stuck her fingers into her ears now and smiled at him.

"It will be unbelievably loud," she said simply.

Around them, *Cerberus* awakened with an angry growl, a desert dragon drawn from its slumber.

Quickly, Emad also blocked his ears, but he found that the sound entered via his bones, a harsh vibration he could not resist.

And then movement.

Cerberus chasing down whatever fool had awakened it, intent on making a morning snack of them. Emad had never felt such power.

Or such potential.

He could see stealing an aircraft.

No, he would need a pilot as well. But he could see the need for something that could range impossibly far and attack the Italian patrols when they thought they were safe, such as laagered up at night. Or strung out in the middle of the sands seeking his men.

Yes, the Senussi needed an air force. Just leaping into the air on the back of a dragon named *Cerberus* showed him that.

What could he do to thwart those Italian bastards from up here?

The noise finally receded as the aircraft reached some sort of altitude. Emad moved to look out the window, but he caught Zareen staring at him with a slight smile. He felt a blush claim him.

In the desert, they wore the shemagh to cover their heads and exposed skin, but he had pulled the scarf back once he was inside.

His entire face was exposed.

Emad wondered what she had seen.

"Thinking about the future," he said, trying to deflect any questions.

"It must have been a happy dream, from your smile," she said, redoubling his blush.

"Liberating my homeland," he said, still not wishing to get into the details of the number of men he might have to kill to achieve that goal. Or the pleasure he would derive from it.

"I understand," she replied with a sudden grimace.

Emad saw through her shell at that moment. Perhaps nobody else ever would, but you had to be the unwelcome child of two cultures to understand belonging to neither. And she was going to liberate Persia from the Russians and the British both, if she could.

However she could.

However many men she had to kill to do it.

What would the world look like if there were no more colonies? Only independent nations founded on cultures, rather than boundaries imposed by treaties hashed out in European capitals?

Would Cyrenaica, Fezzan, and Tripolitania be a workable country? Or should they each remain independent as well? What would the people who lived there desire?

Even the Persian Empire had been broken apart by the Russians carving off slices, until only the plateau itself, the heartland, remained.

Farther afield, would the Indian subcontinent work better as one vast morass of cultures and religions, or should it be allowed to revert into the various lands it had been since time immemorial?

What could they do to make the world a better place,

when the Europeans no longer made the decisions for everyone?

Emad needed the stranger Zareen had mentioned. She had infected him with her dream, even with a few, casual words.

The Man With No Face.

Was he truly an alien being, sent down here from the heavens to witness humans? Or a scout finding exploitable weaknesses?

Emad could not imagine an alien culture advanced enough to travel through space that could not immediately conquer the Earth, if that was their goal, so he had to imagine an ambassador instead.

He would find the man, *inshallah*, and find the truth.

Emad smiled at Zareen with understanding. They both shared a war that was far larger than anyone might imagine.

Dreams.

He looked forward to Cairo.

There was a Frenchman there who perhaps needed to be taught a lesson.

CHAPTER TWENTY-EIGHT

Finn just shook his head at the big Kraut.

"Seriously?" he asked in that quiet voice that wouldn't make it back to the passenger cabin.

Hans grinned, like he did when he was being silly. Because Germans are the most serious people on earth. Just ask one.

"Yes," Hans chuckled. "It will do you both good. Level playing field and all that, like Americans are so fond of."

"You're a nut," Finn said.

"*Ja*," Hans laughed outright and stood up, shifting carefully to his left so he could stick his head back. "Emad, would you care to sit up in the cockpit for a bit? The view is *wunderbar*."

Finn didn't catch the response, but his co-pilot went aft, so it must have been positive.

A moment later, the Bedouin stepped to the doorway and looked around.

"This is the yoke," Finn explained, pointing with one hand while holding it with the other. "Whatever you do, don't touch it. There are also pedals under your feet that control the tail like stirrups on a horse, so watch them when you sit. Make sense?"

"It does," the man replied with that odd, British brogue that wasn't Zareen's accent, nor the guy from the BBC at night.

Finn grabbed the wheel with both hands and made sure he had his feet firmly planted below, just in case the guy did something crazy or stupid.

They were at about nine thousand feet right now, in clear skies with perhaps a trace of a tailwind. There would be time to recover, but Finn would rather never have to do it.

Better safe, and all that.

The man sat on the right with a look of pure awe on his face.

Finn remembered that look, but he hadn't seen it in a mirror in maybe twenty years.

Gods, he was getting old.

Emad looked to be somewhere around thirty, but it was hard to tell, with the way the hot sun sucked the life out of people young.

Blue eyes staring out of an Arab face were just weird.

"Ever flown before?" Finn asked.

"I have not," the man replied. That explained a little of his nervousness. "But now I find myself wondering at what I might do to recruit a small force of planes that might be used to attack the Italians from the air."

"That'll be expensive," Finn said. "Lot of parts to move around, and you'll need something newer than *Cerberus*, with more range, to presumably fly them from a British base. Probably time to start robbing Italian banks."

"Continue robbing Italian banks," Emad laughed now.

"Running any guerrilla operation is a costly proposition, Finn. We cannot tax our own people enough to support us, nor do outsiders provide sufficient funding. It was better before Spain, but that war has absorbed many resources that had once come here."

"Well, the Italians are mostly flying biplanes around here, so if you can get anything even remotely better, you'll be a threat," Finn nodded. "Then maybe something like a Douglas DC-2 to haul freight. Or you could talk to your British friends about borrowing a couple of Vickers Wellingtons to haul fuel and supplies out here. The 416 Wellington Mark IC has the range to haul one hell of a lot of stuff if you refit the bomb bays for cargo but keep the guns against interceptors."

"You seem to have given this a lot of thought, Finn," Emad was suddenly serious. "Are you also anticipating a war?"

"Been expecting it," Finn replied. "Me and Hans have a lot of time up in the air these days, just going from point to point. You get to see a lot of the world when you're in a different place every day."

"And your opinion?"

"Folks are gonna push," Finn shrugged. "Other folks'll push back. Dunno if we'll come bail everybody out again, like last time. But you never know."

"You think the Americans might not get involved?" Emad asked.

"We almost didn't last time," Finn said. "Not until the Jerries sank the Lusitania. Probably take something equally stupid this time, but Hitler and Mussolini strike me as just the fellows for that sort of thing. Maybe the Japs, too. You never know what it will be."

"And how will you react, if it does come?" Emad asked.

Something in his voice had Finn looking over, but the man had a poker face going right now. Smooth and slick, not giving anything away.

"Ain't no colonies in South America, Emad," Finn said with a tone harder than he had anticipated. "Monroe guaranteed that. Maybe them folks traded European overlords for American ones, if my old buddies from the service days are right, but mostly they can do what they want, as long as they don't upset the bankers."

"Which is why you advocate robbing banks?" Emad asked.

Finn shrugged and smiled.

"In the States, those folks are insured by the government, so the little people don't lose money," he said. "Just the fat cats in charge."

"And if I could steal a bigger plane, might I entice you into trading *Cerberus* and flying for me?" Emad asked.

Again, Finn's head snapped around.

The guy was serious. *Starting a war with the Italians* kind of serious. Except he already was in a war with those folks. Had been, all his life, most likely, since Italy invaded clear back before the war.

They've been unsuccessfully trying to conquer the place for nearly thirty years now?

Maybe they needed a little help getting their asses kicked.

"Maybe," Finn offered back. "At some point, somebody's going to want this beast back. Plus, *Cerberus* is largely obsolete these days, doubly so since Ford got out of the business and just makes cars and trucks now. Lot of nicer aircraft on the market lately."

"Then let us get to Cairo and find this Man With No Face," Emad pronounced.

Hans must have known something was up. Something Finn had missed.

Just like the lousy Kraut not to say anything and let folks spring things on him.

But then again, maybe Hans hadn't been sure which way Finn would leap. Not like they'd done much in the last month, besides a couple of joyrides for folks and a few runs to haul some mail.

Most days, Finn had been content to sit in the hammock and let the day slip by.

Damn it, that was a bad way to lose track of a whole life. He was an expert on that sort of thing.

What had he done in the twenty years since the War ended? Dinked around France for a while, flying. Had a wife for a time, but it hadn't lasted. Probably just as well.

Time in the States, doing things he didn't like to talk about with most folks.

Ended up in Italy looking for a job with a bunch of incompetent punks who didn't know how to run a business and left him stranded in Egypt.

Not that he'd done much about it. Not until Zareen had driven up and hired him for an adventure.

Shit, I'm old. And in a rut.

Hans, I'm going to pay you back for this.

Finn smiled at the Bedouin and nodded. He hadn't gotten the whole story about the Man With No Face, other than he was somehow tied up with that wreckage Zareen had found.

He was the ghost waiting for them when they got back to Cairo.

When Finn's contract with the woman was originally supposed to end. Everyone kiss on both cheeks and go their separate ways. That sort of thing.

Except that everyone had already assumed the adventure was continuing. And had maybe forgotten to ask him.

Hans, I'm seriously going to pay you back for this.

Because yeah, curiosity wasn't about to let go of him.

And after that?

Most likely a war.

Be nice to pay a few people back.

Finn looked at Emad with new eyes. The man had just been watching.

Waiting.

Wondering.

Finn understood that.

"I'm in."

CHAPTER TWENTY-NINE

Asher was confident that he had the man's pattern down now.

Humans were creatures of habit, far more so than the Durren. Rise at a specific time each day, despite lacking an impetus. Eat similar food. Smoke only one brand of cigarettes. Drink a specific flavored water.

Asher figured that he could always get a job in advertising, that thing Americans called *Madison Avenue* in the distant land of New York City, if his programming somehow failed enough that he learned how to be bored. His insights into humanity would allow him to manipulate them in ways that would bring Durren vengeance down on him faster than anything.

This must be what evil felt like, then.

He waited outside the hotel where the Frenchmen were staying. The sun had set not long ago, plunging most of Cairo into darkness. The richer neighborhoods, like this one, had occasional streetlights to make them look like Durren towns at night, as well as lights on façades advertising various dreams and evils.

And the organic messiness of the street layout even reminded him of home, so unlike the maps he had seen of French and American cities, dominated by their modern grids, compared to older European places that tended to be rings left over from defensive walls. In Egypt, Asher assumed the original streets had been designed by goats and cattle.

Still, he had to be more careful in this district. British patrols occasionally passed, keeping foreigners safe from the people born here. As well as strangers from other planets.

He had called in a favor to trade his usual robes for something more elegant and middle class, such as an Egyptian gentleman of leisure might wear. It made him less visible than the rattier robes he normally wore. Those for when he wanted to fit in with a different milieu of clients.

His cadre of street urchins had tracked the man named Bertrand here. He was the one who appeared to be a competent killer in the employ of a second man, Didier Beauchêne. Beauchêne was the organizational competence, a French industrialist with fascist leanings.

Asher didn't really understand human fascism. On the face of it, it seemed to promote positive cultural elements of pride and patriotism.

However, in every instance Asher had been able to research, it almost immediately morphed into a systemic oppression against some cultural, linguistic, or perhaps ethnic minority by abuse of authority. Separation into groups, where a group in power used fear of other groups to justify immense and unethical violence, such as the Jews of Russia and Germany, or the Democrats of Spain.

Italy had colonies on both sides of Egypt now, in Libya

and Abyssinia, and Asher had heard many horror stories of the things Mussolini's forces had done. They were even worse than what the British had done for the Opium Trade in Asia or the Slave Trade in the Americas.

Hopefully, the British had finally begun to grow up, although Asher had his doubts there.

Perhaps he needed to work with the Americans at some point, if they could get over their racial issues and recognize a common humanity.

And perhaps the Durren were right and there was nothing that could be done to help the denizens of this planet until they all finally decided to grow up.

Asher pondered how long that might take as he watched the lights in a particular pair of rooms at the hotel across the street.

One was almost always dark, as the one known as Bertrand spent much of his time out in Cairo seeking the Man With No Face, never realizing how close such an elusive creature really was right now.

The other room was almost always lit in the afternoon and evening, frequently with the curtains drawn.

The room where Beauchêne resided, like a Terran spider at the center of its web.

But the man had his rhythms.

His habits.

Dinner every evening, departing his room at as precisely six in the evening as human technology could measure it.

Asher's tools were more accurate, but the human day was the product of a wobbly planet whose spin was slowing over the millennia. If Asher remained here long enough, he might be able to even witness it, but hopefully his reactors would die long before that.

Or the Durren would come to take him home and imprison him someplace more sophisticated than this backwards hellhole.

The lights went out in the window as Asher watched.

He began to move immediately, striding out of this most recent alleyway like a man with a purpose.

Asher had learned that humans accorded such behavior relevance. As one man had explained it, if you looked like a person with a mission, others assumed you were going about it and generally ignored you.

Thus had he dressed well and taken the time to blend in with middle-class Egyptian nightlife.

Across the street, pausing to avoid a rushing truck, Asher ascended the four broad steps that separated the hotel's porch from the street, nodding to the doorman as he approached.

"Good evening," he said in crisp English with just a hint of an Arabic accent.

Again, a sophisticated businessman on the way to someplace importance. Perhaps meeting someone.

Madison Avenue's evil on a petite scale.

The doorman tipped his cap and pulled the door open as Asher approached, allowing him entrance into the vast lobby.

Looking at the fine paintings on the wall and the expensive furniture, this room represented all the wealth that had been extracted from the poverty around him. Even the electric chandelier on the ceiling.

Rather than pause to examine it, Asher photographed everything and turned slightly to his left, circling a small island of chairs back-to-back in the middle as a waiting area and crossing the lobby towards the front staircase. The room had seventeen people immediately visible, doing various mundane activities, including smoking and apparently just waiting.

One man, Egyptian by coloration and larger than most humans in the city, lowered his newspaper and stared flatly at Asher as he walked by.

Asher understood the term undercover hotel detective as a job, and nodded to the man, making it obvious that he wore a mask designed to protect the sensibilities of the innocent, rather than hide his identity from the authorities.

There were an unfortunate number of men in Cairo who had suffered some level of physical damage to their faces that culturally demanded such a mask. It would mark Asher as having been here, were someone to ask later, but the underworld already knew that the Frenchman sought him out.

Some would presume that Asher was coming for a meeting, when news spread, while others would suspect his true motive.

A few would perhaps be disappointed that Beauchêne was not assassinated by the Man With No Face, but those fools did not understand an *Autonomous Simulated Human Exploration Robot* in the first place.

Asher was incapable of harming a human by his very programming.

The hotel detective did not smile, but he did nod in Asher's direction, marking his presence and admitting him as an acceptable guest to be passing through, rather than raising an immediate alarm that would see Asher explode into motion at a ground speed faster than many vehicles were capable of matching over this terrain.

Asher continued walking, ascending the staircase as though he was headed to the smaller restaurant and bar on the second floor, rather than the larger one below. They shared the exact same kitchen and menu, varying only in the staffs supporting each, and perhaps the status accorded the visitors.

He turned right at the top of the stairs and crossed the balcony. Rather than enter the restaurant at this time, he walked purposefully into the men's restroom, chose a stall, and sat to wait.

Below, the hotel detective, had he been following, would eventually relax. Perhaps he would presume Asher had gone into the restaurant when the man wasn't looking.

Robots are nothing if not infinitely patient.

Beauchêne might pass this way as well, stopping here because he normally ate his dinner with the more august guests, so Asher needed to give the man several minutes to settle himself, rather than risk a confrontation in such an awkward and embarrassing place.

Time passed. Asher waited. He was so programmed.

Asher emerged from the restroom and quick-scanned the lobby. The hotel detective was talking to someone, facing away, so Asher moved towards the interior stairs quickly.

Up a flight quietly, he emerged on Beauchêne's floor and counted doors to the correct one. There were no lights under the door, so he approached, boots muffled on the rich, red carpeting.

The locks at this level of technology were laughably simple. Because he was intended for surveillance of the humans without resorting to advanced technology, lock picking had been included in his programming. This lock surrendered to him almost as fast as it would have to the key itself, then Asher was inside, closing the door behind him.

First risk: someone waiting in the darkness for him,

having been alerted somehow by noticing the tribe of juvenile watchers. Neither pistol nor knife would harm his chassis, although there was some concern, as Beauchêne was known to dabble in advanced weapons systems.

Asher was also stronger than a human, so he was not at risk, but his cover would be blown at that point and he would need to abandon Cairo for a generation.

Or forever.

No one awaited him when he entered, so the robot counted that as a victory. No chance of causing injury to a human in an accidental scuffle.

Standard upscale hotel room, with a small bathroom near the front and a closet hung with several matching suits. Larger space beyond with a writing desk and bar for entertaining. Bed tucked off to one side, rather than being in a separate room, as larger suites did on the fourth floor. Door to a balcony with more chairs and a small table, so one could enjoy the evening breezes and biting insects that ignored automatons.

Didier Beauchêne lived almost monastically, from the way the room presented. Bed made. Papers aligned on the desk just so.

The only clue that someone actually lived here was the smell of tobacco in the air and the ash tray overfilled on the writing desk where the man worked.

Asher quick-scanned the exact layout of the desk and began thumbing through papers and effects. The Frenchman had a large journal underneath several other books and piles of paper, so Asher removed it from the pile and photographed each page as quickly as he could turn them. Analysis could wait until later.

Similarly, every piece of paper was scanned on both sides,

before being returned to the exact placement it had had before.

Drawers in the dresser were carefully examined, revealing nothing useful, but Asher also scanned underneath them, where he found something taped. Removing the tape as carefully as possible, he found an envelope containing nearly a thousand British pounds in large notes.

Stealing such money was a juvenile thing to do, but it also allowed Asher the opportunity to materially damage the man's ability to continue his reckless pursuit.

Asher considered making a mess of the room, as though a simple burglar had attacked it, rather than a spy, but the hotel detective would remember his presence, and he had no wish to have the British authorities also pursuing him, if it could be avoided.

He took all but one of the notes and returned the envelope to its place.

Based on a series of detective radio dramas that were broadcast on a wavelength and power he could pick up, Asher also looked between the mattresses on the bed, finding a smaller journal. He scanned everything into memory and returned it.

Moving without a false step had its advantages, as he was able to touch everything in the room, including going through pockets of the suits in the closet and towels in the bathroom, in under five minutes, and to do so in utter silence.

He looked at the room after he had replaced everything again. Had he lips, he would have smiled, but it remained internal for now. He had as much information from Beauchêne as he could get without interrogating the man under threat of torture. Better, the Frenchman should have no indication that his privacy had been violated, at least until he went to extract more money for some task and discovered that he had been robbed at some point.

Asher listened at the door. Hearing nothing, he opened it, quickly looked both ways, and stepped into the hallway.

There was a back staircase that was normally the domain of the staff. Not secret, *per se*, but out of the way and leading to the kitchen and laundry, rather than the restaurant and lobby.

It provided him a way out that hopefully reduced his risks of running into either of the Frenchmen.

He needed time to collate all the data he had stolen.

CHAPTER THIRTY

Zareen watched as Finn lined up *Cerberus* with the runway and began the descent into what her mind kept interpreting as the final showdown with the Frenchman.

Nothing at all had gone the way she anticipated since she arrived in Cairo. First Beauchêne being able to follow her so quickly. Then meeting Finn Severijns and Hans.

Now, Emad al-Sadri.

She wasn't sure what was next, but the two men had come to a bizarre sort of understanding, just bonding up there in cockpit. Zareen would have even considered being offended, but Father had taught her that the two genders both did those sorts of things. It rarely crossed over, but two strangers sitting in a bar having a bottle of wine might accidentally turn into blood brothers, just as two women might adopt one another after five minutes of conversation.

Zareen wasn't sure what Emad's true motives were, but the Bedouin now seemed to understand that Finn and Hans would stand between him and her, right next to Ghada, if necessary. And he had modified his behavior accordingly.

She didn't think the man had courting in mind, not the least because Cairo was just a way station for her, while he was a lifetime resident of Cyrenaica on his first visit even so far as nearby Egypt.

But right now, she had to worry about Beauchêne and the Man With No Face.

What had the Frenchman learned while she'd been gone? Hopefully not much, and she was back several days earlier than she had originally expected.

However, she now had the information she needed to pursue the other man.

To entice him, since she expected that it would be impossible to actually chase the man if he didn't wish to be tracked.

The alien had already survived being shipwrecked on Earth for at least twenty years. Perhaps longer. There was little that even a band of humans could do, unless she decided to bring the entire British establishment in on her secret.

Better to let the man live in peace than that. She would never get the British out of Persia if that happened.

She glanced over at Emad, but he was rapt, staring out the side window at the approaching earth, this being only the second time he had ever landed, and the first just a few hours ago at Kharga.

Zareen had no better idea how to find her target than she did yesterday.

"Landing coming up," Finn called over the sound of the engines and the wind. "Everyone brace."

She was strapped in. Emad settled with his back to the cockpit wall and smiled grimly at her, still getting used to this sort of thing.

Zareen had to remind herself that the man was a Bedouin

warband leader from the deep desert, despite reading Gibran in English.

The wheels touched down as expertly as she had come to expect from Finn and Hans and the plane rumbled down the runway before stopping and dancing lightly back to the far end.

Had it only been so few days since she had first laid eyes on the plane across the landing field? To Zareen, it felt like years, almost.

How strange that trip to the desert had been.

Almost like twelve years in the city of Orphalese.

Finn powered everything down and turned to her with a face shadowed with storms for a moment, before it returned to normal.

"Zareen, you're back to Cairo," he said, as if that was a pronouncement of doom.

In a way, it was, as she had only hired the man to transport her there and then return.

Except...

"I know that this was supposed to be the end of things, Finn," she said carefully. "But I also remember telling you that I planned to spend a week in the desert, digging and exploring. I'd still be interested in keeping you and Hans on the payroll for another few days, if you were interested."

Emad smiled where neither of the pilots could see. Finn glanced over at his German sidekick and got a nod in return.

"What did you have in mind?" Finn asked, smiling now.

"The second half of my planned mission," she said. "All of you know about the wreckage we expect to find under those rocks if we can ever dig."

Nods from the three men as Emad rose and the pilots unbuckled and began to move aft.

Zareen rose as well, making her way to the rear of the cabin so she'd be out of the way.

"In addition, I believe that I have a lead to someone who was on that aircraft," Zareen said, watching all three men blanch in surprise.

"*Das war ein raumschiff*," Hans exclaimed.

"Indeed, I also believe it was a spaceship, Hans," Zareen said. "And there was a pilot. Or at least a passenger. I believe he lives in Cairo today."

Dead silence. Even the insects had stopped chirping and clicking as everyone digested that tidbit of information.

"How do we find him?" Emad asked as Finn opened the hatch and stepped out into sunlight.

Everyone else followed, standing now in a small circle near the tail of the craft as Hans pulled out chocks to securely wedge the wheels in place.

"We cannot," Zareen turned a serious look on Emad. "Many fools have tried, and he melts away like a ghost."

"Which is why you needed to go to Gabal El Uweinat," Finn said suddenly. "He'll want to know what you found, so he'll come to you."

"Exactly," she nodded. "At the same time, the Frenchman and his assassin will also come. I've tangled with them before, even here in Cairo, although I think my shot missed him as he went over the balcony."

"You shot at him?" Emad was surprised.

"And missed," she said, disgusted. "He moves faster than anyone I've ever met and the shot was rushed. Next time I will pause the moment necessary to make sure it takes him through the heart."

"I see," the Bedouin said and closed his mouth.

"So I must bait a trap, here in Cairo," Zareen smiled at

her four accomplices. "Enough honey that we draw in the Man With No Face. At the same time, we will also bring in Beauchêne and his killer, Bertrand."

"I don't like men who threaten ladies," Finn said in a flat, hard drawl that summed up the level of ugly violence the Frenchman might expect, were they to meet.

Hans grunted and nodded.

Ghada was already sworn to her in ways that the men probably weren't equipped to understand.

Emad nodded. Just like that.

Zareen had been prepared to argue with the men. It was still a man's world out there, regardless of her opinions on the topic. She was facing three big men, none of them cowards.

Unconsciously, she had been expecting at least one of them to balk at her.

None had.

All three men had not acquiesced to her, so much as assumed she was in charge and they needed to take her orders. And all of them were much older than her. More mature.

Something.

What a strange and lovely world.

"What do we do first?" Emad asked.

"I will guard the plane," Hans announced to her. "If you are out causing trouble, it is possible that trouble will find us here, so we need this as a secured base from which to operate. Plus, *Cerberus* will need care and attention after the desert dust. I can enlist the Brits to help, so Finn can assist you in town."

That might have been the most words she had heard from the normally taciturn German in one breath. Still, she recognized it for what it was: an offer of help that would secure their rear, while allowing the quiet, introspective man to contribute to their mission and their peace of mind in his own way.

She smiled and placed a hand on his arm.

"Thank you," she said simply.

More was unnecessary. Hans was who he was.

"Okay, so the rest of us need to go into Cairo proper with you and set up a trap?" Finn asked.

"Correct," she said.

"I will stick out like a dandelion in a rose garden," Emad said.

"I'm thinking we'll need to put you in an average suit," Finn spoke up. "Not too nice. Untailored off the rack perhaps. Dress you like a Westerner, at least for now."

"Oh?" Emad asked. "And it will not make me look tacky, when I am around Zareen?"

"We'll tell everyone you're Italian," Finn smiled. "You're already making them look bad. This will just add to it. And someone will underestimate you, considering how most people around here feel about Italians."

Emad laughed brightly as he caught the joke. Everyone smiled.

Zareen took a deep breath.

Now was when things would get interesting.

CHAPTER THIRTY-ONE

Finn was the first to admit that he was a man to hold a grudge. Like, forever.

Even little Charlie Alpin in fourth grade and that one thing with the frogs.

Finn hadn't forgotten.

He was, however, unlikely to be able to track down the men who had actually owned Aurora Italia Airlines unless he made a career of it, and all they'd done was fire him while he was a thousand miles from the nifty little café in Rome where he liked to eat when he passed through each time.

Hell, he didn't even bother with a flat anymore, owning almost nothing personally except a few trinkets stored on *Cerberus* and whatever might be in a trunk that his brother was holding at the house in Billings. If Finn ever made it back there.

But Emad had mentioned a few things about the world while they talked. And Finn knew a few things from living with the Italians for the last couple of years and flying folks around.

Didn't add up to anything nice.

I mean, the British might be stuffy shits most of the time, but they weren't nearly as bad as the Italians had been behaving lately.

And he had maybe finally decided to take sides. It had only been twenty years since he had first decided to help save the world the first time. Maybe he'd been coasting.

Trouble was coming. He'd need to find a way to get Hans a fake passport, either Swiss or American, if things were really going to get as bad as it looked.

They were riding into Cairo now in a nice car that the hotel had sent after Finn had hiked to the main terminal and placed a call. Zareen had tried to do it. Emad had wanted to say something. Neither of them knew who to ask for and how to wheedle a favor.

They also hadn't lived at the airport for the last month rent free, either.

So they had a car now.

Finn found it terribly amusing, watching.

Zareen and Ghada rode facing forward at the rear of the big Mercedes, the model almost identical to the one that German staff cars were built from. He and Emad were facing aft, him across from Ghada and Emad facing Zareen.

Finn refrained from commenting. The man might be a bad-ass warlord from the high desert, but he hadn't spent much time around smart, dangerous women, that much was obvious.

Hell, he probably hadn't blushed this much in his life.

Finn smiled, wondering if this was what *belonging* felt like. He'd been on his own for so long that he'd forgotten.

"What's so funny?" Ghada, of all people asked him.

"Owe the Italians some trouble," Finn said to Zareen's killer. "Never expected it to look like this."

"More trouble than just stranding you in Cairo, Finn?" Ghada asked, maybe already speaking more than she had all of yesterday.

He nodded to both her mistress and the new guy.

"Yeah," he decided. "Man might be able to kind of ignore things when he's just keeping his head down and flying from here to there. You don't really develop roots. Seems like I've missed a few things that maybe should have caused me to say something earlier."

"It is never too late to join a good fight, my friend," Zareen said. "I, for one, am happy to have you with us."

"And I," Emad agreed.

Ghada just smiled at him.

Finn shrugged. Not a lot to say.

"So what happens when we get into town?" he asked the woman in charge.

She was dressed like usual, in those tight jodhpurs that distracted, the white linen shirt that always looked freshly pressed, even after two days in the desert, and that vest.

Zareen had put away the Mauser in her traveling bag, same as he'd tucked the old Colt under the flying jacket for foul weather that he'd dragged out from the back of the plane.

"You two are going to visit a tailor and each acquire a pair of suits that will allow you admittance the nicer clubs. Tuxedos are not yet on the menu."

"Yet?" Emad asked, maybe a little more shakily than Finn would have.

Maybe.

"Yet." She smiled and nodded. "Later. And Finn, while dressing him off the rack might be a good practical joke to play on the Italians, I'd rather you both looked well-presented. And make sure your tailor leaves space for your shoulder holster, as well as doing a two-vent jacket so you can get to a pistol on your hip sometime. Same for Emad. Am I clear?"

"Yes, ma'am," Finn answered.

Woman was in charge. Dangerous. Had the brains. Had the drive. Had the connections. Hell, even had the money.

Finn was kind of looking forward to the first berk who just assumed that he or Emad were in charge of this little commando unit.

Hopefully, Zareen would just cut the fool to shreds with her vocabulary, and not her hands.

Not a woman to mess with.

"Driver, I need you to make a stop," she called suddenly, handing Finn a couple of big Pound bills and giving the man up front an address somewhere that Finn didn't recognize.

He never usually went into town. Just landed out on the edge and there was a car parked waiting next to the fuel truck if folks were coming or going. Maybe a ride to a local hotel, depending on the schedule.

At least in the bad old days.

Running an airplane was an expensive business, so he'd need to find a way to keep *Cerberus* in fuel and parts. Or worse, trade the old warhorse in for a newer model that was faster and had greater range.

The look in Zareen's eyes suggested that she might be planning to make them a more permanent offer on her staff.

Finn wasn't sure how he felt about that. Or what Hans would say, but the big Kraut had an even greater tendency to just go along with things than Finn did. And he liked the little lady, too, so he'd probably be in.

Air Pirates of Cyrenaica?

Weirder way to look at it than what he had been.

Might not suck, though.

The car eventually dropped them on a corner.

"You're three blocks from the hotel, that way," Zareen leaned out the window and pointed, as Finn found himself and Emad standing on the sidewalk.

The crowd was a little better dressed than he was here, mostly Western suits in such a way that he and Emad both stood out, even if many of the folks around here looked Egyptian.

"The tailor behind you is one of the better ones," she continued. "Tell him I sent you and that it's a rush job. He'll understand."

Finn suddenly felt like he'd wandered into a swamp, that patch of what you thought was solid earth where you'd step and suddenly you're in thigh-deep water you never saw, trying not to drown.

Finn nodded, lacking anything intelligent to say to the woman right now.

Ghada winking at him from over Zareen's shoulder just made it worse, but at least he had friends.

The car drove off as Zareen leaned back and Finn turned to his new friend.

"You ready for this?" he asked.

"No," Emad replied. "That's not going to stop us, though."

Finn laughed.

"No, it's not," he said. "There are some bad men out there that need a good talking to."

"Is that why you brought the Colt?" Emad asked.

"Sometimes, they don't want to listen."

CHAPTER THIRTY-TWO

Emad considered the interior of the shop. Wondered exactly how he'd gotten himself into this situation.

Maybe exactly what this situation was.

Somehow, he had stopped being in charge of things and not realized it.

Finn was already dressed in a new suit. He was apparently close enough to a normal size that the tailor had not required much work to fit him. Dark brown suit with a vest he could add but wasn't wearing now. Matching gray suit in a bag, along with his flying attire, such as it had been.

Finn smiled at him now as the tailor emerged from the back room. He had a lighter suit on a hangar and approached like an Emir.

"This will do for tonight," the fussy little man said in a thick, Polish accent. "As Miss Shirazi said that it is necessary in a hurry, I will work tonight on fixing two suits that will fit you more comfortably, and we will trade tomorrow. The jacket is good enough, as you do not require the chest space that your friend does for firearms. You will need a different cut in order to fit your weapon comfortably, although you may wish to consider carrying something more modern in the future."

The tailor handed him the suit and vanished into the back with a murmur that he would return shortly.

Emad didn't ask why the little Polish gentleman seemed to be such an expert on tailoring around weapons. And doing it on the fly. There seemed to be aspects to city life that Emad had missed, going directly from a palace to the wild deserts.

He would need to spend more time in Cairo, it seemed.

And he still had not determined when he was going to go looking for a trained mechanic he could hire or recruit. Neither Finn nor Hans would be on the market, obviously.

At least as long as Zareen needed them.

Had he just taken a new job, as well? He was supposed to be protecting a flank of the desert from his small base but would need a cousin such as Karim to step in if he was going to be gone longer than a few days.

Was it a permanent change? Should he seek out the Emir himself, distant cousin Idris somewhere here in Egypt, and ask for the man's blessing?

Or would that make it worse for everyone?

Too much unknown right now.

At least he had a proper suit. Or two. For whatever reason he might need them.

The tailor returned and handed him a shoulder holster similar to what Finn wore.

"This should fit your revolver for now," he said simply. "Let me see how everything fits before I send you out into society and mistakenly embarrass you."

Emad stripped quickly down to his undergarments and

replaced them with a Western suit that felt alien in ways he found difficult to describe. Like the tie the man had to tie for him was a tentacle strangling the life out of him.

Drowning somewhere besides the sandy sea?

Finn handed him the .455 revolver that Emad normally had on his hip, the big Mk VI a comfortable weight. It slid into the holster well enough and the jacket fit concealed it.

Well enough. He was unused to carrying it this way, and his arm kept touching it and jarring his mind.

"Gentlemen, my shop will be open at ten tomorrow morning," the little tailor told them in a voice like a school master. "You will return then and we will be able to dress you properly for your adventures with Miss Shirazi. Good day."

Emad took it for the dismissal it was and joined Finn out on the street, carrying a small satchel containing the clothes he had been wearing earlier while the other man had a long bag for his clothes.

"Feels wrong, doesn't it?" Finn asked as they turned and headed to where the hotel was supposed to be. "Like you're someone else when you put it on, right?"

"Indeed," Emad had to agree. "I have never worn Western style dress like this."

"I only do when someone's getting married or buried," Finn nodded. "If that's the case, better be that Frog doing it."

"Do you think there will be trouble?" Emad asked.

"Kinda counting on it," Finn grinned. "Look at what we found out there and what people might do for that information. Lots of potential to make new weapons if you can decipher out how to do it. Or find the guy who knows, which is what's next."

"What is next, Finn?" Emad asked as they walked, sobering.

Finn seemed to feel the same, because his face also grew serious.

"Figure that maybe when she's done here, she might be taking her little war somewhere else," Finn said. "Might need some help when she does."

"And you will be there?" Emad asked.

"Don't think she can do it alone," the big American said. "You?"

"That might be more complicated," Emad admitted to the man, wanting to sound him out.

The pilot grinned.

"She'd have told you to take a flying leap if she didn't want you around, Emad," Finn replied. "So you got that going for you."

"And you do not mind?" Emad asked carefully, still unsure of the relationships between the four foreigners.

"Long as you mind your manners," Finn's grin was still there, but it had an edge of menace now. "And understand when to take no as an answer. Rest of it's not my business."

Ah. Yes. Protective, like a brother or an uncle.

He could work with that.

No woman he had ever met had caught his mind like Zareen Shirazi.

CHAPTER THIRTY-THREE

Zareen had listened. Smiled even, and then put her foot down anyway.

She was wearing a nice A-line dress tonight, belted, with short sleeves in blue silk. Ghada was wearing another of Zareen's dresses as they waited in the lobby for the men to arrive, having gotten a call when they left the shop.

"Stop fidgeting," Zareen muttered under her breath to the woman next to her on the couch.

"I can't get comfortable," Ghada hissed back.

"It takes practice," Zareen replied with a grin. "At least you were able to stash your knives. I have nowhere for my pistol in this outfit, unless I want to add a holster for something tiny in a garter belt."

"Why is this necessary?" Ghada asked, still a little disgruntled that she was dressed as a westerner, including pulling her long, black hair back into a braid and even decadently showering this afternoon.

"We have survived the desert adventures, Ghada," Zareen said. "The men are dressing in suits, so I thought we should match them in something simple and dressy for dinner tonight. Tomorrow, we will begin our next round of dances with Beauchêne and the Man With No Face. You can dress as you wish then."

"That will be an improvement," Ghada said in an exasperated tone.

"Perhaps," Zareen countered. "Men are generally simple creatures, Ghada. They will see you in such a dress and paternally mistake you for a weak creature. When I am in a dress, it is almost universal."

"And pants?" Ghada asked, even more distressed. Or possibly disgusted.

"It puts me on a level playing field with them, when I am not trying to distract them," Zareen replied. "You should consider having an entire range of outfits for that very reason. It allows you to disappear when you need, and not when you don't wish to be overlooked."

Zareen was probably better off not knowing what the woman grumbled under her breath, after she thought about it for a moment. No good would come of such knowledge.

And she was distracted anyway. As tailors went, Dobie Kałuża was among the best she knew at working quickly while not losing anything about his immense skill.

Finn and Emad walked in together, laughing at some shared joke and both carrying bags from Mr. Kałuża's shop.

She rose as they looked around, Ghada joining her a moment later. The men turned towards her at the motion.

Zareen rather liked the way both men's jaws dropped open for a moment, before they remembered to close them. The way the eyes got huge in amazement.

Like she had perhaps planned it that way.

She took Ghada by the elbow like best friends and

approached the men. The hotel's manager appeared a moment later, fussy and polite.

"Mr. Severijns, and Mr. al-Sadri," Zareen pointed to the two men, introducing them. "Could you have their things taken directly to their rooms while we have dinner?"

"Immediately, madam," he bowed.

A bellboy materialized as though from thin air and collected bags without a word.

The two men still appeared to be in shock.

It was good.

Zareen dropped Ghada's arm and took Emad's instead. Ghada did the same with Finn. Both women nearly laughed at the comical looks on the men's faces.

"Gentlemen?" She had to draw Emad along, but his mind and manners caught up a step later and he was moving.

She glanced back and Finn was still coming to grips, but he would manage.

Up the staircase, they entered the restaurant, where everything was already arranged, with the best view. Zareen wasn't sure where Beauchêne was staying, but it wasn't here, so the chances of running into him tonight were slim.

Emad and Finn were both armed if that happened.

And Ghada had her knives and fists as well.

She ordered champagne for the table as the waiter delivered menus and left them alone.

"Tomorrow, we will begin stalking our prey," Zareen said.

She spoke mostly to Ghada, because the men were apparently still recovering. Ghada's grin was almost enough to light up the room by itself, but Zareen knew how much the woman was looking forward to encountering Bertrand again after he had broken into their suite.

"Who are we after first?" Finn finally managed, after a drink of water for what appeared to be a dry throat.

"We are after the Man With No Face," she replied quietly. "It is simply a misfortune of life that Didier will probably choose to be in our way, seeking to find out what we have discovered, as well as preventing us from talking to the other."

"If we are back from the desert in only a day, what will that tell them?" Emad asked now.

"Nothing and everything," Zareen smiled serenely. "Perhaps we have already found something so amazing that we had to return to Cairo to get help. Perhaps we were chased away by savage Bedouin tribesmen, the kind who might have followed me all the way to Cairo."

She liked the blush that came to Emad's cheeks. Too many of his cousins were hard, angry men, stubbornly rooted in their sexism and unwilling to grant a woman even equality, let alone superiority.

Emad al-Sadri seemed to be cut from a different cloth altogether.

"And perhaps I have given up in the desert, having spent all of a whole day looking around and not seeing anyone waiting for me," Zareen continued with droll sarcasm. "I doubt Didier is foolish enough to fall for that, but he might mistake my return for mere flightiness. If he does, then it puts us at an advantage. He must find out what I know, so he must come to us."

"Will he be able to react quickly enough to our return?" Finn asked.

"If I believed that, I wouldn't have chosen to take a night off with Ghada and moved to celebrate," Zareen said. "We would be upstairs ordering room service and planning a campaign for the next war."

"Gotcha," Finn nodded.

Zareen noted the way his eyes kept straying to Ghada, seated on his immediate left, rather than her across from him. She kept her smile secret.

Ghada was not one to blush, either, but had done so more in the last few hours than in all the years Zareen had known the woman.

Besides, tonight was intended to be one she spent off duty. To celebrate her new-found friends, and perhaps recruit them onto her team more permanently, if possible. Both men, all three men, brought unique skills and experiences she would probably need over the long haul.

Because her war had only really just begun.

There was so much to be done.

CHAPTER THIRTY-FOUR

Dinner had been amazing. Better than Finn had probably eaten in years. It wasn't that he was cheap, so much as a man with simple tastes. That café in Rome was great food, but really just northern Italian peasant food for the most part. Tuscan, with local flavors thrown in.

Tonight he had eaten steak in a yellow, creamy curry that the Brits had brought with them from India. Spicy, tangy, and sweet, all at once. A couple of bottles of champagne had left everybody loose without overdoing anything.

They were taking a bit of a walk as a constitutional after dinner. This was one of the nicest neighborhoods in Cairo, as near as Finn could tell, so they weren't the only ones about, although it was really just now dinner time, so there wasn't much traffic around. The few folks he could see were Westerners, rather than Egyptian, and there were more cars parked just on this street than he'd seen in the last week, out at the airstrip.

And Ghada seemed okay with holding his elbow. She was a few inches taller than Zareen, and curvier. Not lush like a

Rubin, but more interesting compared to her boss, who had a nice ass, an average waist, and almost no chest.

Ghada had filled out that shift in much more distracting ways. And tonight's dress was tight across her body in ways that Finn found a little befuddling.

Ahead of them, Zareen was walking on Emad's arm like they had been courting for years. He wasn't sure what made them so comfortable together, except that she was half English and half Persian, and he had some similar background to have been born with blue eyes.

Maybe they were just both well-bred outsiders in their own world? Made as much sense as anything.

"Top three thoughts?" Ghada asked out of the blue as he was wool-gathering.

"Huh?" he managed rather brilliantly.

"What are the top three things you keep thinking about as you go quiet, Finn?" she explained.

"Oh," he managed the second time. "Let's see. How'd I end up in Cairo? How'd I end up with a beautiful woman on my arm? Where's the adventure go next?"

She had really cute dimples when she smiled. Finn wasn't sure he'd seen them before now. Thinking about it, she'd always been dour and focused, so maybe a little loosening up was a good thing for her as well.

A car suddenly pulled to the curb and a man had a gun pointed at them out the back window before Finn could react and reach for his own piece.

Ghada had stiffened as well, but he wasn't sure where she'd hidden those knives she'd had with her earlier. Wasn't sure he wanted to see.

Well, maybe he did, after all. Weren't many places she could put them out of sight in that outfit. And he'd already seen more of her than was probably acceptable in polite company.

"Miss Shirazi, so nice to see you again," a man said as he stepped out of the far side of the big Mercedes and pointed his own weird-looking gun at everyone. Too small to be lethal, except that he was holding it like it might be.

Finn had no idea. Didn't feel like getting shot right now to find out.

"Didier," Zareen snarled in that polite way that only the British have ever seemed to manage.

Like Finn and Ghada, she and Emad had been caught off guard by a French bastard who got the drop on everyone.

Turned out that maybe he had indeed had enough spies in Cairo to know as soon as they landed? It had only been a few hours, so somebody had blabbed.

"Yes, my dear," Didier Beauchêne said.

Finn assumed that this was the guy she'd been talking about.

"I'm going to need you to accompany my associate and I," the Frenchman said. "I have some questions I'd like to ask you. Don't move, boy."

That last at Emad as he had apparently tensed.

Bad idea, Emad.

Finn knew he couldn't get to his own Colt faster than he'd get shot, and he was used to drawing and firing that way occasionally.

"Talk?" Zareen asked. "You?"

"Just talk," Didier replied. "We've been allies against others in the past. I propose a similar alliance now, but I'd like to talk in a place where you don't have all your killers with you. Get in, and I'll return you to the hotel in a few hours."

Wasn't much anybody could do at this point. The guy on the near side of the vehicle had a mad-dog kind of smile on his face and a compact automatic of some sort that Finn couldn't identify. Zareen had said that the Frenchman invented weapons, so it might be anything.

Anybody moving suddenly and someone would be dead pretty quick, even if the two Frenchmen were put down a few seconds later.

Finn cursed inwardly.

He was back in Chicago again, dealing with those South Side punks and a load of illicit hooch.

Zareen knew a bad hand when she saw it, too.

"Very well, Didier," she said, carefully removing her arm from Emad's. "Let us talk and see what you know that might be worth trading for, after what I discovered in the desert."

"Not alone," Ghada suddenly said, stepping away from Finn and nearly getting shot when the other guy (Bertrand?) suddenly aimed at her.

If he'd been thinking, Finn might have moved and drawn.

And maybe gotten someone killed.

"You wish to accompany your friend and leave your gentleman behind?" Didier asked in a superior tone.

"Are you a threat to a woman's honor and dignity?" Ghada asked. "Someone should chaperone."

Finn didn't grin, but he wanted to. Most of the time, Ghada had a soft Persian accent to her words, regardless of the language she was speaking.

Right now, she sounded just like her mistress, that London posh accent with a bit of a Scottish burr underneath that just screamed money and breeding.

Apparently, Finn wasn't the only person who didn't

recognize Ghada out of those desert-wife robes she normally wore everywhere, because both Frogs flinched.

And no Frenchman likes to be called a cad, or anything along those lines. Especially not by a beautiful, exotic woman.

Finn watched the storm clouds on the boss man's face gather, then disperse in an instant.

"Very well," he snarled, stepping a little clear of the rear door. "Both of you walk around the rear of the vehicle and enter. Both men step back against the building and don't do anything that requires Bertrand to shoot you. Am I clear?"

"You are," Emad said.

Finn was grinding his teeth.

However, the complicated choreography played out well enough. Both women moved one way. He and Emad moved the other.

The killer's mad-dog smile never wavered. Didier watched like a master of ceremonies, following the women into the back of the vehicle and closing the door.

The big car revved and raced away. Finn considered racing after it, but short of opening fire on the car and maybe hitting one of the women in his madness, there wasn't much he could do.

From the angry scowl on Emad's face, he was having the same thoughts.

"Now what?" Emad asked after a moment to compose himself. "Will he hurt them?"

A figure stepped out of a nearby alley and approached. Finn had the big Colt out and centered on the guy's chest so automatically that he didn't even realize what he was doing until the safety was thumbed off.

"I believe the two women are in grave danger," the man said, ignoring the weapon.

Finn looked closely.

The man wore the sorts of robes that rich Arabs did around here, with a hood up that shadowed things.

He didn't even flinch at the gun in his face, but instead came to a serene rest six feet away.

"Who are you?" Finn demanded, finger on the trigger and ready to blow the bastard away.

Slowly, carefully, deliberately the man reached up and flipped his cowl back, revealing one of those old-fashioned theater masks, with a small hole for breathing and two eyeholes that had been covered over with gauze or something so you couldn't see his eyes.

The rest looked like it had been made out of steel by a master jeweler and finished with enamel, almost like those Japanese masks Finn had seen.

"I am the person you have been looking for, Finn Severi-jns" he said. "The Man With No Face."

CHAPTER THIRTY-FIVE

Asher knew that the weapon could not really harm him. A Colt Officer's Model 1911 .45 ACP fired a projectile that was frequently subsonic, depending on the powder load. As force was just mass times vector, it would flatten itself against his metal frame and possibly leave a small stain of lead and copper he would need to buff out later, having damaged his robes in passing through.

The .455 Webley Mk VI, a breech-loading revolver the other man drew, was probably even less dangerous.

Asher considered suggesting that these men should upgrade their personal arsenals at some point, but now was not the time and he wasn't sure his programming would technically allow it. He would need to find a delicate way around those prohibitions, he feared.

"I'll skip all the boring parts," the man Severijns began, his barrel never actually wavering by enough that a human could detect it. "How did you find us and what do we need to do to rescue the women if they are in danger?"

"I have been tracking you since Miss Zareen Vüsala

Shirazi came to town two weeks ago and began asking about me," Asher replied. "Last night, at about this time, I trespassed into the hotel room currently being maintained by a Mssr. Didier Beauchêne and made copies of all of his documentation, after which I then spent the evening collating them into my own database for stochastic, predictive methodologies."

"Was any of that English, pal?" the American asked.

"I spent the evening understanding your adversary, Mr. Severijns," Asher said flatly. "My calculations and theories of human behavioral norms suggest that Miss Shirazi is in grave danger, as is Miss Attar."

"Who?"

"The other woman with you this evening," Asher said, wondering if he could give the human equivalent of a put-upon huff, lacking lungs to make the reverberations correctly.

"Ghada?" Severijns asked.

"Correct," Asher answered. "I believe that you must rescue them, and do so now, before it is too late."

"Who in Hades name are you, anyway?" Severijns asked.

This pistol wavered some, but that was distraction. The other man held his own weapon perfectly still with a rage so pure that Asher wasn't sure he had ever encountered it among the species.

Asher considered his options. His programming did not allow him to simply write Miss Shirazi off as collateral damage in whatever war those two humans were undertaking.

At the same time, Asher had come to understand that his presence was becoming known outside the narrow rings of Cairo's slums, and that he would need allies.

Thus, the need to dismantle every note, suggestion, idea, and path of rage and vengeance the man known as Beauchêne had carved through various criminal underworlds. Shirazi had done nothing of the sort, according to those humans Asher had been able to interview on the topic.

He absolutely needed allies.

Egypt would not be sufficient to hide him now, as the modern world was intruding and bringing with it outsiders with the sorts of growing technological sophistication that would eventually uncover him.

"If I may?" he asked the humans, holding up his hands to his face.

"Go ahead," Severijns growled.

The other human, the one that Shirazi had apparently brought back with her from the desert, did not speak. He was Arabic, but had blue eyes, so his recent ancestry presumably included a northwestern European.

Asher reached up and detached the mask that concealed his identity from the cloth that he maintained around the rest of his head, hiding the dull, gray metal parts. He lowered it now and watched both men flinch in surprise.

"A robot?" Severijns asked.

"*Autonomous Simulated Human Exploration Robot,*" he replied. "Asher, if you will. It is as good as any other name."

"An alien?" the other man spoke now, his voice gone quiet with surprise.

His pistol never wavered.

"An exploration unit," Asher corrected him. "An electronic life form. All the organics on the ship were killed in the crash and fire."

"So that was your ship we found?" Severijns asked.

"Wreckage, perhaps," Asher nodded. "I thought I had

buried it sufficiently, but the desert winds can be capricious. What did you locate?"

"Piece of glass," Severijns said. "A window a little bigger than my whole hand, rectangular with metal still riveted to it on one side. Too light for anything I'd ever seen. Too strong, as well."

"Yes," Asher agreed, replacing his mask now. "It would be. Gentlemen, I need your help to rescue the women, because my programming forbids me from harming a human, and I fear that violence will be necessary, rather than just the threat thereof."

The two men took a moment to look at each other and a nod passed.

"Let's do it," Severijns said gruffly. "Where did he take them?"

"There is a warehouse," Asher said. "According to the notes I stole from the man, that is the most likely location, as he would not risk a confrontation where there might be witnesses."

"How do we get there?" the stranger asked.

"I have access to a sedan," Asher said. "A Mallory four-door. By what name should I address you, sir?"

"He's Emad," Severijns said. "I'm Finn."

"Emad. Finn," Asher nodded to them. "Shall we?"

They nodded back and Asher began to move, walking at a relatively rapid pace for a human, but both of them kept up. Two blocks over, he found the vehicle as Mahmud had left it for him.

"Can you drive this?" Finn asked.

"Adequately, but without skill," Asher answered.

"Gimme the keys," Finn said. "I'll drive. You ride shotgun. Emad, you're in back on his side, where you'll balance the weight."

"Shotgun?" Asher asked, aware of some colloquialism he had not encountered before. Possibly an Americanism.

"Passenger front," Finn said. "Mallory's an American car, so the driver's on the left. You're on the right."

"Noted," Asher said, handing Finn the keys and moving around the vehicle.

He set his search algorithms on the colloquialism and located a reference to stage coaches in the American West of the late 19th Century. *Shotgun* in this usage indicated an assistant to the driver, armed with such a weapon to be used against bandits pursuing the vehicle.

Bizarre, but within parameters for humans. And Americans tended to be rare in Egypt, so perhaps he would have the opportunity to expand his databases with Finn's help.

They entered the vehicle and Finn started it expertly, roaring away from the curb as Asher called up his map and began offering navigational suggestions.

CHAPTER THIRTY-SIX

Emad felt like a fool. He should have been better prepared. Cairo had distracted him with lights and noise, and he had allowed himself to be lulled into a false sense of security by the others.

He studied the figure seated in front of him, but outwardly the man looked normal enough. Then again, if Zareen was correct, the Man With No Face had been hiding among them for more than twenty years now, and doing so successfully enough that nobody had mentioned it.

Only a few seekers had even uncovered hints.

Emad wasn't sure why the man had revealed himself now, but he also understood how lonely it might be, spending all that time in an alien place as an outsider. He could appreciate that. Zareen would as well.

Both of them existed in places where they did not really belong, outsiders marked by the locals and tolerated but not necessarily embraced. Had the Grand Senussi not accepted him and his mother, Emad wasn't sure where he would have ended up.

Perhaps a Cairo slum like the one they drove through now at a reckless speed? If anyone but Finn was driving like this, Emad would have been nervous, but he had watched the man fly *Cerberus*.

"Asher, are you truly an alien?" Emad asked as they tore through the street.

"Was I constructed on another planet?" the creature replied. "Certainly. But I am not alive, as humans understand such things. This unit is perhaps a more sophisticated machine than that in which we ride, but I bear a closer kinship to it than I do to organic creatures such as yourselves."

"Then why emerge now?" Emad pressed. "Why reveal yourself?"

"People are preparing to do violence to each other over me," Asher said. "I cannot use violence in my own defense, but Zareen Shirazi should not be put at risk, merely for asking questions. Plus, I suspect that I will need allies in the future to maintain my secrecy from the greater world. Having weighed Beauchêne's motives and plans, I made a conscious decision. At least as conscious as I am capable of emulating."

"And if we do violence on your behalf?" Emad asked.

"I was programmed to weigh my own outcomes, Emad," the man said. "This is perhaps the fundamental definition of a lesser evil, as human philosophers have explored such a thing. I cannot return to my home at present, so I must either make accommodations to coexist with humans or cause this unit to cease operating in such a way that it remains hidden for all time from human discovery. I have considered walking into the middle of one of your oceans, for example."

"What're you doing after we rescue the women?" Finn spoke up now.

"That remains to be seen, Finn," Asher replied. "Miss Shirazi impresses me with her capabilities and intent in ways that most humans do not. Once she is safe, I will reassess things."

Emad didn't like the way the situation had occurred, but perhaps Zareen had an extra benefactor that the Frenchmen had not counted on. They had promised no harm would come to the two women, so he couldn't just shoot them both like rabid dogs, but they would need to be on their best behavior when he caught up with them.

If one of them *had* harmed Zareen, no depth of any hell would be enough to protect that man from Emad's vengeance.

CHAPTER THIRTY-SEVEN

Finn didn't know this area of Cairo, but then he really didn't know any of them, when you got right down to it. Just vectors on a map and distances that *Cerberus* could fly on one tank of gas.

Hell, until a month ago, he'd never been in Egypt longer than four days transiting.

But the robot had fed him directions with a certainty that Finn found amazing.

"You got a map of the place?" Finn asked.

"I have traversed every alley and street in Cairo at least once in the last three years," the robot said in a calm, Egyptian voice tinged with an English accent that had to have been faked. "My cartographical records are probably an order of magnitude more sophisticated than any the local authorities have access to."

"A simple yes or no would have been sufficient," Finn snapped at the man. Creature. Robot.

"Yes, Finn," the thing said.

Asher. His name was Asher. Or something. Good as any.

"How close are we?" he asked Asher.

"Approximately one mile," Asher answered.

"Could anybody else get here as fast as we did?" Finn asked.

"Only an expert," Asher replied. "I calculate that such a person would have arrived at the destination two minutes ago, assuming this was their goal. I can be wrong about their intentions, but this was the preeminent option in Beauchêne's notes."

"Good enough," Finn said. "We can't just drive right up and kick in the door. We'll need to scout the place."

"Agreed," Emad spoke up from the back seat. "Find us a spot to park when you get close, then I'll handle that. Asher, I presume you would prefer not to accompany us into violence, but your help would presumably improve the odds that we could enter and rescue the women without resorting to violence."

Finn grinned. Trust the sneaky Bedouin to work his way long ways around the robot and talk him into helping them raid the place. Fellow hadn't been the least worried that he might get shot.

In the movies and comics, that usually meant that they were bullet-proof. Of course, bullets came in lots of different sizes.

If he was going to be running around with bullet-proof robots, maybe he needed to go back to something like his dad's old cowboy .44 Colt. Or find himself something heavier. Everyone was moving to the silly, little 9mm Parabellum these days, at least in Europe. Americans still preferred the .45.

Tommy gun, maybe? Bigger and a heftier punch.

Maybe something silly instead?

Finn turned that last corner and pulled the car alongside a warehouse as Asher directed him. It was evening and mostly the streets were quiet here. He killed the car and looked over at the other two.

"I fear you are perhaps correct, Emad," Asher said. "I am programmed not to do physical violence, but they may not know that. And my sensors are more sophisticated than yours, as well. I will accompany you."

Finn nodded, pocketed the keys, and climbed out, drawing his Colt again.

Not quite OK Corral, but maybe Tom Mix or Gene Autry, depending on who was writing the script. He had a hell of a situation on his hands, but hopefully the other two understood how to fight dirty.

Finn doubted that the Frenchman would be all about the Marquis of Queensbury. Especially not if someone kicked in the door on him.

He glared at the other two, changed it into a smile as they got into character with him, and started down the street towards the warehouse where Asher thought the women were.

Time to go back to his bootlegging days.

And maybe he'd end up having to shoot someone.

Again.

CHAPTER THIRTY-EIGHT

Zareen scowled, but there wasn't much she could have done from the moment that Bertrand leaned out the window with his pistol, prepared to shoot anyone or everyone. Had Ghada been in her usual attire, she might have gotten her knives out and possibly thrown one, but Zareen had convinced her to dress like they'd been on a double date.

It had been a successful one, too. Right up to the moment when Beauchêne had showed up.

She found herself in what looked like an abandoned warehouse as the car rolled to a stop. They were out on the western outskirts of town, well away from the river and almost facing the desert. Around her, the wood beams holding the ceiling up looked rickety and ancient, as though the place was centuries old, when it was probably a few decades at most.

Poor, available, and cheap, most likely.

"Sit here," Beauchêne commanded them as they got out of the Mercedes, both men pointing guns at them unwaveringly.

She didn't recognize the driver, but he had obviously been hired by Didier, as he just parked the car inside the warehouse, then got out and closed the garage door before returning to the front seat. She saw a flash of light and smelled the tobacco as the man lit a cigarette and blew smoke out the open window of the vehicle.

There was a single electric light overhead, but the space was vast and gloomy, so Didier lit a match. Suddenly a kerosene lamp was filling the space with more light.

Zareen was directed to a wooden chair. Ghada was seated next to her and Bertrand suddenly had her hands behind her and tied together to the frame. Ghada started to move, but Didier had his pistol almost touching her chest, so she subsided.

The other woman was quickly trussed as well.

"Good," Didier said, holstering his weird little pistol on his hip, under his jacket. "Now, my dear, we need to talk."

"This is hardly what I agreed to, Didier," Zareen said mildly. "It does not bode well for any sort of alliance that you tie me up like you are going to torture information out of us if we don't talk."

"Not immediately, Zareen," Didier replied ambiguously. "I wanted your undivided attention. Since your friend chose to join you, this keeps the two of you from doing anything stupid while I ask some questions. It's really in your best interests this way, you see?"

"If those are the lies you tell yourself to sleep at night, Didier," Zareen smiled cruelly at the man. "Did you ever locate the Man With No Face yet?"

She watched the man's face suffuse with rage for a second, before clearing as she distracted him.

Thank you, Father, for your lessons on negotiations and how to rattle someone without them realizing it.

"I have not," Didier replied. "We have begun to search, but he fled as soon as we started. I have not had sufficient time to quarter the entire city that I might locate him. I was also expecting you to be gone for a week, rather than two days. What happened out there? What did you find?"

"The Bedouins do not take kindly to company," Zareen replied, carefully shading the truth around as she needed it. "We were captured less than six hours after we arrived at our dig, held overnight, and then ordered to depart. It took until the next morning, so that we could leave safely. They are hard men, but not barbarians. But that is absolutely their desert."

"So you found nothing?" Didier asked.

"I didn't say that," Zareen turned on the charm now. "Those tribesmen weren't able to understand my gear, so I was able to hide something."

"What?" the man demanded, eyes threatening to bug out of his head now.

"Part of an aircraft, perhaps," she said ambiguously. "None that I am familiar with, but my cover story with the tribesmen was that I was seeking wreckage of an experimental German craft. This might have been such a thing had they found it."

"There are no German aircraft, experimental or otherwise, anywhere near Egypt," Didier sneered.

"Ah, but they don't know that," she smiled. "I brought it home with me from right under their noses."

"You did what?" He had started to pace, but turned back to her now, his face white with shock. "Where is it?"

"Hidden," Zareen said serenely. "Nowhere you'll find it.

So you should be nice to me, Didier. Perhaps I'll show it to you."

"So it exists?"

"I believe so, Didier," Zareen said, turning serious now. "Enough stories from enough disparate sources corroborate to give me a high degree of confidence, even if the desert is too dangerous for us to go dig in, at least without taking a small army along first."

"There really is an alien, walking among us?"

Didier seemed more shocked than angered now, as she watched him. But then, she had been working with only vague clues, drawn from reports from three different colonial empires that did not like one another. None of the pieces spelled it out, at least until you placed all the notecards onto a table and started drawing lines between them.

"Why else would he work so assiduously to hide?" Zareen asked.

She had pondered long and hard on that very topic.

It made no sense for one alien to arrive secretly, unless he was a spy, seeking out humanity's weaknesses. For the ship to crash and strand him here gave a certain credence to his subsequent behavior, but again, someone should have come back for the man at some point.

It had been twenty-some years. Had they presumed everyone aboard the craft was lost?

She did not know, but what human could understand a truly alien mind?

"So we know that the Man With No Face is an alien?" Didier mused aloud.

Bertrand stood off to one side through all this, smiling like a feral cat just waiting for the mouse to emerge finally from its hole.

Zareen did not have pleasant expectations, but she had made one of the greatest mistakes of her young life tonight. If she got out of this one, she would never be so badly equipped or ill prepared again.

"We suspect," Zareen turned her attention back to Didier.

Ghada would be focused on the assassin. Of that she had no doubts.

"I cannot see how you expect to have any greater success at catching him than I do, my dear," the Frenchman sneered at her.

Tried to sneer, anyway. It didn't help matters that he was only taller than her if she wore flats and he had dress heels on. Bertrand was as tall as Finn or Emad, but Didier was a plump butterball of a man. An intellectual, not a warrior.

She had to be both.

"Ah, but I don't have to catch him," Zareen countered, deciding to play one of her trump cards now. She needed better leverage with the Frenchman. "I plan to draw him to me, if he will come."

"How?" Didier demanded.

"I have part of his spaceship," Zareen smiled, reminding the man that it was hidden and he might never find it if he hurt her. "He will want to know what I've learned from my sojourn into the desert. You catch more flies with honey than vinegar, after all."

He flinched under her words, as intended.

No man likes a woman to remind him of his shortcomings. Especially not one who prided himself on his intellectual superiority, like Didier did.

"And he'll come to you, just like that?" the man snapped.

"Perhaps," she shrugged as much as her bindings would

allow. "He may have already fled Cairo due to your bumbling, Didier, so we may have to start from scratch, wherever he heads next."

"Well, then, my dear, perhaps it was time that we moved on to more persuasive arguments," he said.

She watched him nod to Bertrand, who put away his pistol and drew a long knife with a terrible smile.

The assassin took one step and then froze as a voice emerged from the shadows behind her.

"Son, I'd think long and hard before I did anything stupid right now."

CHAPTER THIRTY-NINE

Finn could tell that the warehouse was kind of a dump. But then, the whole neighborhood was, so he didn't figure he should be surprised. At least they were on the desert edge of the city, so he could tell he was in the right place, looking down at the tire tracks disappearing into the garage door on this side.

Still crisp. Sand a little damp to the touch when he knelt to check it. Driven over not that long ago, or the wind would have stirred things up.

He was back in Montana stalking elk with his dad and brother again, twenty-five years ago. Before a war intruded.

"There's got to be a door other than this," Finn said, pointing at the garage door itself. Opening that was about the dumbest way he could think of to sneak up on someone.

"There is an office door around the right corner," Asher said.

The alien robot fellow ended up in the middle of their line as Finn led and Emad brought up the rear. Weird, but probably for the best right now.

Finn slipped to the corner and looked around it.

It helped that the evening was getting along at this point. Even the hardest working folks had gone home for dinner, leaving the streets around here pretty empty.

That would be useful if this ended up in a firefight shortly.

Sure enough, plain wooden door.

Finn moved down the wall like a ghost as the sun was just about gone.

Simple thing when he got close. Round, brass handle long since black with air and age. Deadbolt above that.

Finn tested the handle. It turned smoothly enough, but the door was bolted, which he expected. Only a fool left a door unlocked in Cairo's slums.

He could probably kick the door in pretty easy. Wood frame would splinter under a boot, just like in the old days running rum. Even a strike plate wouldn't help much, considering how much rage he was feeling in his soul right now.

"Perhaps I can be of assistance?" the robot spoke quietly, like an accountant running quarterly numbers.

"Be my guest," Finn said and stepped back to watch.

Asher pulled a pair of metal bits from a pocket and slipped them into the deadbolt above the lock. It almost looked like the robot was twitching, but the whole thing turned a second later.

Hell, Finn wasn't sure he could have opened the damned thing that fast with a key in his hand.

He'd never had to learn the art of picking a lock. Boots were usually faster, and in those days the folks on the other side usually needed to be surprised by gunmen.

Asher stepped back. He looked to have been smiling, if

he had a lips over that steel jaw of his. The mask just conveyed his amusement.

Still, pretty useful fellow to have around.

"How sneaky are you, Finn?" Emad asked now.

"What have you got in mind?" Finn asked the skinny Bedouin.

"A desert stalk," Emad grinned. "Much like I did to you that first night."

"When you got right under me and dumped me on my ass while I was asleep?" Finn grinned back.

"It was a useful way to control the situation, my friend," Emad grinned even broader.

Finn stepped to one side and indicated the door.

"All yours."

Emad turned deadly serious in a heartbeat as Finn watched. Like a snake that had just woken up from a good sunning on a south-facing rock.

"I lead," he said quietly. "Then Finn. Asher, you may wish to remain outside, since you cannot harm humans, or you can join us if you wish."

"I would rather see the situation unfold," Asher said. "I need to make decisions about my own future as a result of this evening."

"So be it."

Finn watched Emad close a hand on the handle and turn it. The door opened inward silently, just enough for Emad to peek in, and then slip into the gloom.

Finn had a thicker chest, so he had to push the door just a little farther to open it, and then the robot followed, closing the portal behind him.

They were in a small office, but from the dust and crap piled up on the desks and counters, it had been abandoned a long time ago. Voices came from the warehouse itself through an open door on the far end of the room, so Finn followed Emad that direction.

The Frenchman and Zareen exchanging barbs, for the most part.

At the doorway, Emad knelt down, so Finn slipped up behind him to spy the room.

Driver in the Mercedes off to one side, smoking a cigarette. Two Frenchmen standing in the middle of the only light, near a table. Two women looked to be tied up in chairs in front of them.

"Thoughts, my friend?" Emad whispered into Finn's ear as he rose.

"Not feeling especially charitable today," Finn growled quietly back, listening to the tone of the conversation.

"I shall eliminate the driver first," Emad said quietly. "Then we will confront the others."

"Got you covered," Finn replied.

The Bedouin slipped out of the door like a breeze coming up, vanishing to the left as Finn focused on the side-kick over there. The short guy wasn't holding a gun, but the other one was.

He'd need to go down first.

Finn listened to the conversation, trying to gauge his moment.

"Perhaps," Zareen replied to something languidly. "He may have already fled Cairo due to your bumbling, Didier, so we might have to start from scratch, wherever he heads next."

"Well, then, my dear, perhaps it was time that we moved on to more persuasive arguments," the pudgy Frenchman replied.

The short guy turned to his sidekick and nodded. That

fellow put away his pistol and drew a long knife with a terrible smile that Finn didn't much like.

Finn slipped through the doorway as the assassin began to move towards the women.

"Son, I'd think long and hard before I did anything stupid right now," Finn growled loud enough that everyone understood he'd fire first and maybe not bother asking any questions later.

Colt was dead-centered on the lanky one, but Finn was prepared to pivot and kill the boss if that man did something foolish afterwards.

Might as well add Egypt to the places with warrants out for his arrest, after all.

Everyone else's heads turned as the car door on the big Mercedes opened, but Finn figured that Emad had that area covered. Fellow was damned sneaky, and the tall one over there still had a knife in his hand.

"Drop the knife buddy, before I kill you," Finn commanded. "One. Two."

The knife thumped into the floorboards satisfactorily.

"Hands over your heads, both of you," Finn continued. "I'm assuming you have guns, and I'd be fine shooting both of you and then disarming you while you bleed to death on the floor in front of me. Am I clear?"

Gods, this brought back too much of Chicago, but that town had at least turned a simple farm boy into the sort of dangerous adult that could be doing things like this in Cairo.

"How did you find us?" the short one demanded angrily.

"I got a lot of friends in Cairo, pal," Finn smiled. "Best you keep that in mind."

The driver had emerged carefully from the car and

walked over to his boss, hands also in the air as Emad had that big, nasty-looking Webley at his back.

Finn began to walk closer. Not too close, but enough that he didn't have to yell unless he wanted to.

"So I figure that you fellows haven't done anything yet that *requires* me to kill you," Finn grimaced. "At least from the way things look right now. How's about you keep it that way, and we'll call it good?"

"What are you talking about?" the short Frog growled.

"Emad, you got the ladies?" Finn asked, ignoring the question, except to make sure that six hands stayed above three heads.

Tall, skinny fellow was dying first if anything happened. Hell, if anybody *breathed* wrong. Finn would take his chances with the other two, but they weren't killers.

"I do, Finn," Emad said.

Finn trusted the Bedouin at this point. Fellow'd proven his competence more than enough times. And his reliability.

Throw in Hans and they had a pretty good Three Musketeers thing going, especially if you looked at Zareen as d'Artagnan.

Zareen came into view now. Ghada popped up a moment later.

Finn's Colt never wavered.

"Finn, I'm going to disarm them," Ghada said carefully.

"Be my guest," he said, still centered on the one called Bertrand.

Ghada was damned good at this thing, too. She got a pistol from the driver, and then a couple of things from the short one.

He really liked the way she took the boss's gun and put it

right up against Bertrand's side as she got close. Touching his chest with her finger on the trigger.

Any movement and he'd be bleeding out.

Her other hand pulled a pistol and tossed it to Zareen. Two knives came out of various places, meaning he had at least three stilettos on him when this started.

All the weapons got confiscated.

"As Finn said, you didn't technically reach the point where I have any grounds to be more offended than your poor manners around a lady, Didier Beauchêne," Zareen called out in a tart voice, pointing Bertrand's gun at the man. "At the same time, I think that under the circumstances, I shall have to forego the rest of your hospitality. I'm sure you'll understand. If you come up with a reason that we should talk again later, you can send me a cable or something."

"What she's too polite to say right now is that if we ever see any of you again, we're gonna just open fire and assume it was self-defense," Finn said loudly. "You understand my position, boys?"

Tall asshole had a scowl that might etch steel, but he was also outnumbered and unarmed right now.

Finn did like the way Ghada turned back to the tall one, as if she had something she had forgotten to say earlier.

Before anybody could react, she drove a fist into the man's belly so hard it folded him in half with a whoosh of air and collapsed him to the floor like a half-empty sack of grain.

Ghada helpfully picked up that third knife before anybody did anything stupid with it.

"This is not the end," Didier Beauchêne snarled, even as Finn heard the rest of his friends cross behind him and exit through the office.

"Maybe not," Finn smiled. "But it is an ending, and let's just take it all at face value."

He turned and fired a shot into the nearest tire on the Mercedes, killing it nicely, since they'd probably have to completely replace it, rather than just a patch job. Car had a spare, but that would be an hour getting put on. He and the gang would be long gone by then.

Finn turned to the three men and backed away, glancing enough to make it to the doorway.

Once he was through, he slammed the panel shut and threw the little deadbolt. Wouldn't do much besides make one of them kick it in.

He turned and saw the others at the outer door, so he started to jog in their wake.

The ladies were wearing pumps, but not doing that bad of a job. Finn figured that this was the last time he'd see Zareen or Ghada dressed nice. Tomorrow, back to boots and pants and guns.

Shame, that, but Cairo was kind of a rough place, and folks needed to take care of themselves.

"Who is this?" Zareen finally asked as the five of them got back to the Mallory.

"A friend who helped us save your butts from whatever that one fellow had planned," Finn said. "Everyone get in and we'll sort it out. Don't want to be around if trouble's coming."

They piled in and he got the beast started. Somehow, Emad, Asher, and Ghada ended up in the back seat and Zareen was up front with him. Finn dropped it into first and popped the clutch with a swirl of sand and smoke.

Zareen turned and studied the fellow behind Finn.

"You understand that we have been searching for you, correct?" she asked.

"Indeed, Miss Shirazi," Asher replied calmly as Finn listened. "Both you and Didier Beauchêne have shards of a greater whole, and threaten my peace of mind with your further seeking."

"And yet you came to rescue me?" she continued, reminding Finn of a barrister seeking an opening in somebody's alibi.

"I am not capable of harming humans, either by action, nor, more importantly, by inaction, Miss Shirazi," Asher answered. "I have read all of Beauchêne's notes on the various campaigns and battles the two of you have fought over the last three years. Yours is the more honorable side, as much as someone like me might be able to discern such a thing."

"How so?" she pressed as Finn got them around another corner.

"Hey, we going to the hotel?" he asked out loud.

"Yes," Zareen said. "Long enough to pack and haul everything to the airstrip where *Cerberus* is stored. From there, we will make decisions."

Finn nodded and lapsed back into silence.

"Sir?" Zareen asked, but it was obvious she was talking to the robot.

"Fascism is a system that will fail," Asher said quietly. "It appears useful in organizing an industrializing society, but it will then merely lock things in at a low social development score. Humans need greater freedom in order to develop to a stage where they might be contacted from the outside."

"And you do not represent contact, sirrah?" she asked.

"I was intended as an observer, Miss Shirazi," Asher

answered. "A short-term mission to try to understand the current state of human culture."

"But something went wrong, there in the desert."

"Indeed, Miss Shirazi," he said. Finn could even detect some glumness to the robot's tones. "My ship suffered a catastrophic systems failure, crashing and exploding. All the organics aboard were killed instantly. The organic shell encasing me would have allowed me to move among you without notice, but it was burned off, leaving only my robotic frame. Thus, I am forced to live as the Man With No Face, a scholar and oracle in the souq, still trying to fulfill my mission."

"Could you not rebuild your shell?" Zareen asked.

"I am a sociologist, Miss Shirazi, not an engineer."

"And when will your people return for you?" she probed.

"My mission was secret and illegal, Miss Shirazi," Asher said mournfully. "Contact with humans is proscribed, at least until you reach a more advanced social state. Nobody knows I am here, so nobody will come to rescue me. My choices are to do my original mission, or simply end myself in such a way that your kind cannot learn the truth. I chose the former. I continue to choose the former, for at least as long as I can. Now, I appear to be committed to helping humanity uplift itself past any number of potential pitfalls and bottle-necks that might end you as a technological species."

"End us?"

She was shocked. Finn was, too.

"You stand at the cusp of developing weapons of such great devastating power that you could kill the biosphere of this planet, Miss Shirazi," Asher said. "Without the equiva-lent social advancement that would render them unnecessary and unwelcome."

"But you choose to help?" she asked.

"As much as my programming will allow," Asher said.

Zareen lapsed into silence for a moment.

"We will talk more later," she finally said, turning back to face the front.

Finn stole a glance at the woman, but he couldn't tell what she was thinking.

He drove.

CHAPTER FORTY

The *Autonomous Simulated Human Exploration Robot, Mark Seven*, considered his options as Finn Severijns drove the vehicle across the runway at the airstrip where the aircraft known colloquially as *Cerberus* was parked, currently guarded by the German pilot/mechanic Hans Fertig.

His world had changed.

A few days ago, all Asher had to look forward to was what could best be described as entropy. The eventual breakdown of his mechanical systems that required he destroy himself sufficiently to leave no clue for primitive humans to understand.

That was still an option.

At the same time, he was stranded on this planet until someone came along to arrest him, impound his datacore, and then end him as a functional exploration unit.

That thought left him hollow. He had come to like humans.

Most of them were a well-socialized species that looked out for one another and helped when they could. If a terrible few exploited existing systems to rise to dangerous levels of power, that represented a failure of their legal and social systems to prevent such a thing, rather than a default setting.

Humans were growing up. Perhaps at a frightening speed technologically, all things considered, but that was the nature of the particular industrialization path they were on, where competition to create better weapons did indeed spin off social advancements.

Even Asher was not entirely sure why he had gotten involved with Finn Severijns and the man he had finally been introduced to as Emad al-Sadri, a distant cousin of Idris of Cyrenaica.

Except that Zareen Shirazi was in danger, and he was the only sentient being in a position to do something about that. Did not all of his programming *demand* that he become involved at that point?

And what should he do now, besides remain involved, at least from a quiet standpoint?

Was it his mission now to help all of humanity? Certainly, they were poised on the brink of a cataclysm of social destruction that would probably make the so-called Great War pale by comparison.

Could he mitigate that? Did his programming allow him to adopt all of humanity as a thing that should be protected against destruction?

The Mallory sedan came to a rest and everyone exited the vehicle. Asher stood next to the driver's entrance as Finn handed him the keys. Ghada Attar and Emad al-Sadri began removing trunks from the rear. A second vehicle had joined them from the hotel, delivering more equipment on a flatbed.

"The guy you borrowed it from will need it back," the American man said simply. "Thank you for your help."

"It was indeed my pleasure, Finn," Asher replied.

Zareen Shirazi strode close now.

"What will you do next?" she asked. "I doubt Cairo will be safe for you for some time, but there are other cities where you could hide."

"I could, Miss Shirazi," Asher said. "I have not yet reached a conclusion about what would be the best course of action for me."

"My mission has not changed, Asher," she said. "I now know that there are in fact aliens that have visited Earth, but I will continue to seek out what evidence they have left behind. Some of it will help us advance technologically, but that will be necessary to defeat the evil that would reach out its hand over humanity if we do not stop it."

"I cannot contribute to a war, Miss Shirazi," Asher tried to deflect her.

He was not prepared for the smile that appeared on the woman's face.

"How many languages do you speak or read, Asher?" she asked innocently.

"Several hundred," he said automatically. "Including many no longer understood by any living creature."

"And you do not think that is a useful skill for a researcher?"

Asher paused, feeling like his entire datacore had just reversed polarity on him when he wasn't looking.

"I am a scholar..." he started to say.

"And I could use a scholar of your brilliance, Asher," she said. "You are not the first visitor, obviously. I doubt you will be the last, either. How many others have there been?"

"I was not programmed with that information, Miss Shirazi," Asher managed.

Was this what it felt like to stand on the edge of a cliff and look down?

"Would you like to find out?" she asked, still smiling.

Asher paused. He had never known his internal systems to fluctuate like this before, running wildly like an over-revved internal combustion engine with no load on the transmission.

"I would," he decided warily, wondering what manner of excitement and adventure a poor explorer robot like him had just signed up for.

She held out a hand for him to shake in the human, Western European method.

He took it carefully, wondering what it would feel like as a simple glove over his metal appendage.

"Thank you, Miss Shirazi," he said quietly.

"Call me Zareen," she smiled.

READ MORE!

Be sure to read all the books in the Air Pirates of Cyrenaica series!
https://www.knottedroadpress.com/product-category/
science-fiction/air-pirates-of-cyrenaica/

ABOUT THE AUTHOR

Blaze Ward writes science fiction in the Alexandria Station universe (Jessica Keller, The Science Officer, Phil Kosnett, etc.) as well as several other science fiction universes, such as Corsac Fox, Operation Marrakesh, and more. He also writes odd bits of high fantasy with swords and orcs. In addition, he is the Editor and Publisher of *Boundary Shock Quarterly Magazine*. You can find out more at his website www.blaze-ward.com, as well as Facebook, Goodreads, and other places.

Blaze's works are available as ebooks, paper, and audio, and can be found at a variety of online vendors. His newsletter comes out regularly, and you can also follow his blog on his website. He really enjoys interacting with fans, and looks forward to any and all questions—even ones about his books!

Never miss a release!
If you'd like to be notified of new releases, sign up for my newsletter.

http://www.blazeward.com/newsletter/

Buy More!
Did you know that you can buy directly from the KRP website?

ABOUT KNOTTED ROAD PRESS

Knotted Road Press publishes dynamic fiction set in exotic locations and unique non-fiction voices in genres such as autobiography, business, cookbooks, and how-to. Our authors cover a wide range of genres including science fiction, fantasy, mystery, literary, and poetry, appealing to all readers. We offer both DRM-free ebooks and print books for a global readership.

Knotted Road Press
www.KnottedRoadPress.com
www.KnottedRoadPress.com/Shop